SECOND CHANCE AT LOVE

Some years before, after the premature death of her fiancé in an airplane crash, Martia Stapleton plunged into her nurse's training with the determination to let work and a career wipe out her loneliness and heartache. Because of her own tragedy, she developed an intense awareness and a deep sympathy for lonely people and more or less drifted into geriatrics work. Sunset Acres, a retirement village on Florida's Gulf Coast, offered the nurse an ideal opportunity to practice her specialty, always remembering that the way to avoid again being hurt by love was to forswear it. But the latter philosophy was alien to the doctor with whom she was assigned to work, and who saw in Martia not only a competent nurse, but also the ideal woman for whom he had been searching.

SECOND CHANCE AT LOVE

Peggy Gaddis

Gadd.

CURLEY LARGE PRINT
HAMPTON, NEW HAMPSHIRE

1/94 Chivers 17.95 B

Library of Congress Cataloging-in-Publication Data

Gaddis, Peggy.
  Second chance at love / Peggy Gaddis.
    p.   (large print) cm.
  ISBN 0–7927–1791–0 (hardcover)
  ISBN 0–7927–1790–2 (softcover)
  1. Man–woman relationships—Florida—Fiction.
  2. Nurses—Florida—Fiction.
  3. Large type books. I. Title.
[PS3513.A227S33 1993]   93–5486
813'.52—dc20   CIP

British Library Cataloguing in Publication Data available

This Large Print edition is published by Chivers Press, England, and by
Curley Large Print, an imprint of Chivers North America, 1994.

Published by arrangement with Donald MacCampbell, Inc.

U.K. Hardcover ISBN 0 7451 2042 3
U.K. Softcover   ISBN 0 7451 2054 7
U.S. Hardcover ISBN 0 7927 1791 0
U.S. Softcover   ISBN 0 7927 1790 2

Printed in Great Britain

TO
MARY L. MERCER, R.N.,
DeKalb General Hospital,
Decatur, Ga.

In grateful acknowledgment of her friendly,
warm-hearted services while I had the good
fortune to be her patient.

SECOND CHANCE AT LOVE

CHAPTER ONE

Martia Stapleton came out of the long low building, with its proud sign, 'SUNSET ACRES HOSPITAL AND CLINIC,' and stood for a little, gratefully breathing in the fresh, fragrant, salt-tangy air.

The sun had just set, but the scene was still bathed in the golden afterglow. The waters of the Gulf across the road were silver-blue in the golden light, the long, slow ripples coming in almost soundlessly to splash against the sea wall. From above the village the faint scent of orange blossoms from a grove in that direction was wafted to her, faintly tinged with the salt tang of the Gulf. The two tall poinciana trees on the lawn were rose-gold, and the ground beneath them was a carpet of fallen blossoms. The hospital itself was bedded in hibiscus that was practically always in bloom. Down the walk and circling the drive were oleanders. Somewhere near her, a bird sang sleepily and was still. Along the street leading to the village itself, tall palm trees rattled their fronds in a breeze from the Gulf that was never quite still.

Martia breathed deeply and let her shoulders sag wearily. It was all so still, so beautiful, so peaceful. And then she caught

1

her breath on a little sigh of exasperation as two feminine voices broke out ahead of her. They were at it again, she told herself, and for a moment was tempted to turn back to the hospital and hide from them. But she braced herself and went on down the walk.

The two old women who sat on one of the benches beside the drive broke off their bickering, and one of them said, 'There she is now! I knew it was about time for her to go off duty.'

They stood waiting for her, and as she approached them, one of them came hurrying to meet her.

'Miss Stapleton, we've been waiting to talk to you,' she announced, and turned to look with a scowl at the other woman, who merely smiled smugly and clicked her false teeth.

'What's wrong with you two now, Miss Mary? Hello, Miss Lucy. Why didn't you come to the hospital and ask for me?' Martia said.

Miss Mary's plump face hardened slightly.

'Because Dr. John doesn't like us coming to the clinic unless we're really sick,' answered the self-elected spokesman of the two. 'And of course we're not.'

She flung a disdainful glance at the other old woman, who said with venomous sweetness, 'No, of course we're not really sick, except of each other.'

'And that we truly are,' snapped Miss

Mary.

'Now, now, now,' Martia soothed them as though she had been talking to two quarreling children.

She drew the two women back to the bench and sat down between them.

'Now suppose you tell me what this is all about,' she suggested pleasantly.

'Well, Lucy got a letter from her daughter today with a post office money order in it, and all I said was that if Monica was that fond of her, I didn't understand why she didn't visit her now and then,' Miss Mary announced.

Miss Lucy bristled furiously.

'And I reminded her that Monica is a fashion model in Paris and that she can't afford to take time off and make an expensive trip here to visit me,' she flashed. 'After all, she did pay for my apartment here, and she sends me money every month. And I reminded Mary that her son lives in Philadelphia and could get leave to come and visit her any time he wanted to.'

Miss Mary flashed back, 'He has a wife and a couple of children.'

'Whom you've never seen,' Miss Lucy interposed neatly.

'Well, I have pictures of them, and they send me Christmas gifts and birthday cards,' Miss Mary snapped.

Martia put out her hands, laying one on

3

each of the bickering women, and said gently, 'Do you want to know what I think?'

The two old women turned eager, expectant faces to her.

'Of course we do,' they chorused. 'That's why we wanted to talk to you.'

'I think you two have lived together so long that you have gotten on each other's nerves,' Martia stated flatly.

They stared at her in dawning dismay.

'But where else could we live?' Miss Mary asked.

Martia said thoughtfully, 'Well now, let me see. There's Mrs. Gunderson, who has a whole bungalow to herself and who has been very lonely since her husband died a few months ago. I'm sure she'd be very glad to have either of you come to live with her.'

The two old women looked horrified.

'Why, she'd drive a person crazy in no time at all!' It was Miss Mary, the more volatile of the two, who first found her voice. 'Why, she goes around all draped in black and bursting into tears every time she mentions her husband's name; and claims she has dreams of him that she just knows are visions, telling her he is waiting anxiously for her to join him!'

As though she had not heard, Martia went on, 'And then there's that nice Miss Laura Settles, who would so much like a companion to live with her because it's so

4

lonely now that she has retired from teaching school.'

It was Miss Lucy's turn to be horrified. 'Oh, not Miss Settles. She's so brisk and energetic that it tires me just to talk to her. She keeps boasting about what perfect health she has, and she's so impatient with anybody who has an ache or a pain—'

Martia said briskly, as she stood up, 'Well, at the moment I can't think of anyone else. But I'll check the records in the morning. I'm sure I can find acceptable quarters for you so that you need not live together any longer.'

The two old women stood up, too, and Martia saw their hands join together as they faced her.

'Oh, but, Miss Stapleton, we *like* living together,' they chorused. And Miss Mary added breathlessly, 'Why, we've been friends for years. It was because we were such good friends that our children bought this place for us and sent us down here. And we love it! Why, we're as comfortable and snug as two bugs in a rug. We just couldn't be separated now.'

'But you are always quarreling,' Martia pointed out.

The two old women exchanged grins, and Miss Mary answered, 'Well, yes, I reckon we do argue quite a bit. But after all, what other fun is left to us but to wag our tongues and snap at each other?'

Miss Lucy chuckled and slipped her hand through Miss Mary's plump arm.

'Come on, Mary. I'll treat you to dinner at the Inn, and we'll celebrate Monica's check,' she offered.

'But the cats—' Miss Mary protested.

'Fiddle-faddle! We'll feed the cats when we get home,' said Miss Lucy firmly. 'Time they were learning not to be so fussy about their food. And if they get good and hungry, they won't be.'

Over their shoulders, they said a gay, 'Good night, Miss Stapleton, and thanks.'

Martia stood where she was and watched them swing briskly down the walk to the street and then toward the village. Before she could resume the walk to her own quarters, there was a masculine chuckle behind her, and she turned, startled, to see Dr. Peter Hayden standing there, his hands sunk deep into the pockets of his sports jacket, his eyes amused.

'So that's why they call you the listening nurse,' he commented, his dark eyes warmly admiring, his tanned, good-looking face touched by a smile.

Martia smiled back and lifted her shoulders in a slight shrug as she turned to walk on and he fell into step beside her.

'Well, most of these geriatrics patients really need somebody to listen when they feel

6

they need to talk,' she admitted. 'They are lonely and away from those they love, and their minor aches and pains aren't really minor at all. They're very real to them, and no pills or medicines are going to relieve them. They just need to talk to somebody who will listen.'

Dr. Hayden nodded and looked down at her as he walked beside her.

'That's not only good psychology but good common sense,' he approved. 'When I discovered that you were really what Dr. John called you, the perfect nurse, I felt you were wasted just being a sort of listening post. But now that I have come to know you better, and the work of the clinic has been lightened by your services to them, I have changed my mind. You aren't wasted at all. You are doing a very real job and one that is badly needed.'

A little startled by the warmth in his tone, Martia looked up at him swiftly and murmured, 'Why, thank you, Doctor.'

'Praise where praise is due,' he assured her, the grin deepening on his tanned face. 'Since we are both off duty for the evening, how about dinner? Not at the Inn, but somewhere along the road where we won't see a geriatrics patient.'

'I'm afraid not tonight, Doctor. But thank you—'

'Some other time, then?' he persisted,

puzzled by a note in her voice that had almost indicated panic.

'Oh, yes, of course, some other time,' Martia answered him, and hurried up the walk to the nurses' dormitory.

He watched her until the door had closed behind her, and then, with his hands doubled into tight fists, rammed deeply into his pockets, he muttered just above his breath, 'So go ahead and run, my darling. But it won't do you a bit of good. For I can run, too!'

Inside her tiny room in the nurses' dormitory, Martia sat on the edge of her bed, her face in her hands, her shoulders shaking. For she realized how much she was beginning to like Peter Hayden, and she knew that he was beginning to like her, too. And that mustn't happen! She would not fall in love again, because she knew with bitter clarity how much love could hurt when you lost the one you loved.

For a moment, sitting huddled there, she let memories wash over her. She had kept them out of sight, locked fast behind a secret door in her heart, rarely letting even the picture of Derek's face come before the eyes of her mind. But now, at the realization that she was in grave danger of falling in love with Peter Hayden and that he was already on the verge of being in love with her, she opened that secret door, and memories flowed about her.

The joyous morning when she had completed her nurse's training and passed the state examinations and received her cherished cap and pin, Derek had been on a training mission at the air base in Texas and had been unable to attend the graduating services. But he had telephoned her, and had sent an extravagant basket of flowers. And then, in the midst of her happiness and her eager plans for a future she would share with him, had come that shattering telegram. Derek's plane had crashed, and Derek had died in the flaming wreckage.

There had been a period of utter blankness which she could not even remember. Nor did she want to. She had moved like an automaton in a world of smothering darkness, until at last she had come out into a grayness of perpetual twilight and slowly and painfully had come to realize that her only hope lay in devoting herself to her work; dedicating her life to helping others; doing what her profession had taught her to alleviate pain and misery. For she had faced, in that gray twilight, the fact that with Derek's death had gone all her dreams and hopes of happiness and marriage.

She would guard herself, she had determined, against ever falling in love again. She couldn't, because her whole heart had

9

been given to Derek.

Until now there had been no danger of forgetting that determination. No man had appealed to her—until now! Peter Hayden, from her first meeting with him, had made it very plain that he found her definitely attractive. But other men had found her attractive in the eight years since Derek's death, and she had been able merely to laugh at them and go on her way, completely untouched. But now—she drew a long hard breath and clenched her hands tightly before her. Now she was finding an odd new warmth in her heart that had so long been frozen and empty. Now she was feeling a quickening of her pulse when she came face to face with Peter Hayden in their work at the hospital.

Mentally she cried out despairingly, but I don't want to love him, or any man! I don't want to love again!

And far down in her heart a small, persistent voice said quietly, Oh, don't you? Then what are you going to do about it? Run away from him as you have run before? Leave the hospital, find work somewhere else? That's the only way you can avoid seeing him daily, almost hourly. Where will you go?

She loved her work here. But, she reminded herself tautly, she would love nursing anywhere a good nurse was needed.

And without a shred of conceit, she knew herself to be an excellent nurse.

She put her face in her hands and wept soundlessly, as she had not let herself weep since that terrible time eight years ago when news of Derek's death had first reached her.

CHAPTER TWO

Jason Weathersbee jerked the clean sheets about him, refusing to admit even to himself how comfortable it was to be neatly tucked between clean sheets. Of all the indignities that had beset him since his heart attack two weeks ago, the worst was being bathed in bed by two little snippets of nurses and having his linen changed by them while they rolled him neatly this way and that to get the sheets completely smooth and very tidy.

He had never had a serious illness before, one that had kept him bedridden so that he could not even bathe or shave himself. And he was sixty-eight years old.

The door opened, and a small frightened nurse's aide came in with a small pad in her hand. As she approached the bed, she reached for the thermometer in its jar beside him.

Jason scowled furiously, his long, homely face bleak and unfriendly.

'And what the devil do *you* want?' he snarled at her.

'Just to take your temperature, Mr. Weathersbee, and your pulse,' she stammered. 'Open your mouth, please.'

'Get out of here!' snarled Jason furiously.

'Not until I take your temperature, Mr. Weathersbee,' she insisted, and added impulsively, a note of entreaty in her voice, 'Please, Mr. Weathersbee. I've just completed my training, and this is the first time I've been allowed to make rounds on my own. If you don't let me, I'll get a stiff call-down, and maybe I won't be allowed out alone for a long time.'

Jason's scowl faded slightly and he said ungraciously, 'Oh, all right. But let's get it over with.'

He opened his mouth, and the aide popped the thermometer beneath his tongue and put slightly unsteady fingers on his wrist. When she had completed her task and carefully entered figures in her small book, she beamed down at him happily, her dark eyes glowing behind her neat dark-rimmed glasses.

'Thank you, Mr. Weathersbee.' Her voice was warm with gratitude. 'You're not nearly as bad as they say.' Too late she clapped her hand over her mouth, gave him a terrified look and scampered out of the room, remembering to close the door silently

12

behind her.

For a long moment Jason lay still, staring at the closed door, and then he chuckled grimly.

So they think I'm an unholy terror, do they? Well, that's good. Maybe now they'll let me go home, he told himself with satisfaction.

It was perhaps an hour later that Miss Laura Settles, tall, spare, her white hair neatly combed and brushed, came along the corridor, peered at the name on Jason's door, nodded to herself, tapped lightly and, without waiting for answer from within, pushed the door open and came inside, smiling at Jason.

'Good morning, Mr. Weathersbee,' she greeted him brightly.

Jason glared at her. She wasn't a nurse; her crisp summer frock of blue and white checked gingham told him that.

'Who the devil are you?' he snarled at her.

Miss Laura was settling herself beside the bed, obviously intending to stay awhile. She carried an armful of newspapers and magazines, and her smile was bright and warm.

'I'm Laura Settles, Mr. Weathersbee,' she told him. 'I've come to read to you.'

Jason's snarl had turned almost into a roar when he answered, 'Read to me? My dear good woman, I'm quite capable of reading to

13

myself.'

'Of course you are,' Miss Laura soothed him. 'But lying flat on your back, it might strain your eyes. And Miss Stapleton tells me you are not yet allowed to sit up. I brought the Atlanta papers and some news magazines.'

'Well, you can take them right out with you,' snapped Jason. 'I asked for a private room because I wanted privacy. And I'm getting about as much as goldfish in a bowl, what with people popping in and out of here all day, then waking me up at night to give me a sleeping pill or to take my blood pressure or some other fool thing. Now get out!'

Miss Laura only settled herself a little more comfortably in the blue leather-covered armchair and studied him thoughtfully, her eyes very bright behind her neat rimless glasses.

'You really do have a bad temper, don't you?' she observed at last.

'Madam, my temper is my own affair.'

'Oh, no, it isn't,' Miss Laura protested. 'It makes your blood pressure rise, and that's very bad for some one who has had a Stokes-Adams attack.'

Jason glared at her, slightly surprised.

'You're not a nurse. How did you know what kind of heart attack I'd had?' he demanded.

14

'Oh, I asked Miss Stapleton, as I always ask her about any patient I'm going to visit,' Miss Laura told him pleasantly. 'I wouldn't think of calling on any patient who was seriously ill or in pain. But she said you would probably like to have me read to you. I read very well, you know. It's a thing schoolteachers have to learn.'

He was studying her now, his interest caught in spite of himself.

'So you are a retired schoolteacher.'

Miss Laura laughed.

'Most people say they can take one look at me and guess it,' she told him, quite undisturbed, and unfolded the top newspaper. 'Now, what would you like me to read to you? The stock news, I suppose?'

'I don't want you to read anything to me,' Jason thundered at her. 'I just want you to get out of here and stay out.'

Miss Laura dropped the paper and studied him for a long moment. Then she sighed and made a little gesture.

'You *are* lonely, aren't you?' she asked quietly.

'Lonely?' he barked at her. 'I only want privacy.'

Miss Laura nodded thoughtfully.

'That was what I thought I wanted when I first came to Sunset Acres,' she told him. 'I took my savings and bought a small house with a garden, because I'd always wanted to garden. I love flowers. But I soon realized that after all the years when I was so busy teaching school, had friends who dropped in now and then, and attended various school affairs, being alone was a very lonely business. Oh, I have made a few friends here, but it's still lonely living all by myself. I've always had perfect health, so I looked around for some sort of hobby that would help me get through the days. And Dr. John said that I could come and visit the patients here and read to them and do little services for them that the nurses and the aides are too busy to do. It's a way I have of showing my gratitude for the perfect health I've always enjoyed.'

Jason had listened to her in growing astonishment.

'So this is your hobby? Paddling around the hospital, thrusting your unsolicited company on people who are helpless to defend themselves from your unwanted ministrations?'

Miss Laura caught her breath as though he had struck her brutally, and a faint pink rushed into her gaunt, withered face. She stood up, assembling the papers and magazines neatly in her arms, and he saw that her hands were trembling slightly. Her head was high and her eyes were frosty.

'Is that the way it seems to you, Mr. Weathersbee—that I'm a meddlesome old woman sticking my nose in where I'm not wanted? I'm sorry if that's the way it seems. And I promise you faithfully I'll never bother you again!' Her voice was faintly shaken, edged with deep resentment, as she turned and marched out of the room.

'Serves the old witch right,' he growled to himself, trying to deny the feeling of shame that tugged at him. 'Well, maybe I *was* a bit rough on her, but what's a man to do to keep from being invaded by do-gooders? A hobby! Phooey!'

But somehow the day seemed unusually long. Even the aide who brought his lunch merely set it on the tray before him and vanished without conversation.

Disgruntled, Jason ate the lunch and thrust the tray out of his way. He had wanted to be left alone, he reminded himself, and it was apparent that he was going to have his wish.

He was dozing uneasily when the door opened again. This time it was the nurse he knew was called the listening nurse. He eyed her curiously as she approached the bed, a small medication tray in her hand. She offered him some pills in a tiny plastic cup, and Jason accepted it, glared morosely at the contents and sneered, 'What, only three this time? You're cheating me. But I must say it's a pretty color combination: purple, pink and green.'

Holding a glass with a plastic straw in it,

she helped him drink. And then as she put down the glass, she grinned at him and said, 'Oh, you should see what I just took Mrs. Brundage. Five, and a lovely combination of colors.'

'I'll bet,' Jason growled. 'You're the nurse they call the listening nurse, aren't you?'

Martia laughed.

'Makes me sound like a character in a "whodunit," I'm afraid.'

'I hear people talking about the way you soothe people by just listening to their tales of woe, their imaginary problems and illnesses and such.'

'Well, sometimes it helps just to have somebody listen while you talk things out,' Martia reminded him.

'Like psychoanalysis, I suppose.'

'Well, perhaps, though I've never studied psychiatrics,' she admitted. 'It's just that soon after I came here, I found that a good many of the out-patients weren't really ill; that more than anything else they needed somebody to talk to, somebody who would listen. They were lonely and bored. Retirement isn't always easy for people who have always been active and busy.'

'You think I don't know that?' he snapped.

Martia studied him gravely for a moment.

'I'm sure you know it very well,' she answered gently. 'That was why I had hopes that you and Miss Laura might find each

18

other companionable.'

Jason glared at her.

'I don't need anybody to read to me,' he snapped.

'Well, perhaps not, but Miss Laura needs to be needed! It's very important to her. After teaching school for almost forty years and being a very important person and needed in many ways, it's very difficult for her to realize that she isn't needed by anybody at all. That's why she came here to the hospital and begged us to let her help in any way she could. She is so grateful for her rugged health that her heart goes out to others less fortunate.'

'Well, I've always had rugged health, too,' he began.

Martia's slightly mocking smile silenced him.

'Oh, sure,' she told him lightly. 'Only you drove yourself relentlessly, piling up money, building up a big business, letting your temper control you. And then your nephews managed to finagle the business away from you, and you went broke.'

Jason was glaring at her furiously.

'And then,' Martia went on, 'you let your hatred of them and your fury take control of you until you wound up with a heart attack.'

'Well, what would you have done?' he blazed at her. 'Given them a pat on the back, thanked them for the miserable pittance they flung you as they would have flung a bone to a hungry dog and stuck you off down here, giving you your choice between being committed to a mental institution or being imprisoned in a retirement village?'

Martia said quietly, 'I'd hardly call a hundred thousand dollars a pittance, Mr. Weathersbee, and we are very glad you chose Sunset Acres instead of a mental institution, but I still think that you could recover much faster if you would stop hating your nephews. You can't afford it, Mr. Weathersbee.'

His glare was part fury, part bewilderment.

'Afford it?' he repeated, obviously unable to understand her meaning.

'It takes a lot of energy, Mr. Weathersbee, to hate,' she reminded him. 'And you don't have that much energy to waste.'

He was obviously outraged, yet also intrigued.

'You think it's a waste to hate people, to resent the way they have treated you?' he demanded.

'Of course,' Martia assured him. 'Don't you?'

'I suppose I'm expected to forgive my enemies, love them that persecute me?' he sneered.

'The Bible says so,' she reminded him.

He made a disgusted gesture that was filled with contempt.

'Oh, the Bible was written thousands of years ago; it doesn't apply to the present-day world,' he snapped.

'That is your opinion, Mr. Weathersbee, and you're entitled to hold it,' she told him seriously.

'Well, thanks!' he snapped. 'Thanks a whole lot.'

Martia turned toward the door, looking over her shoulder at him to say pleasantly, 'Well, I'll be in to see you later, Mr. Weathersbee.'

The door closed behind her, and Jason lay staring at it thoughtfully.

For the rest of the afternoon, those who came in and out of the room to tend him found him so quiet, so lost in thought, that they left the room puzzled, wondering what had happened.

Late in the afternoon, Dr. John Hamilton, head of the staff of the hospital, came in to see him.

'Hello, Jason.' Dr. John, an old friend, came bustling in and sat down beside the bed. 'What's all this I hear about your fangs being drawn? You're not scaring people nearly as much as usual.'

Jason turned on him a look that was strangely meek.

'Sorry I've been such a nuisance, John,' he mumbled unwillingly.

Dr. John's plump, ruddy face expressed

astonishment.

'Why, Jason, I don't think I've ever heard you say you were sorry about anything before, and I've known you since we were boys,' he said. 'Even the lab technician who came to give you your E.C.G. said she didn't have a bit of trouble with you. And usually you fight like a bay steer when she starts in.'

'John, do you think I should forgive the boys?' Jason demanded flatly.

Thoroughly startled, Dr. John stared at him, bushy gray eyebrows raised.

'Now where did you get that idea, Jason?' he asked.

'You ought to know—from whom but that nurse you all call the listening nurse?' Jason growled, abashed now and more his accustomed self. 'She claims I can't afford the energy it takes.'

'Martia Stapleton is a fine nurse, almost, I'd say, the perfect nurse, and I've never heard her make a statement that didn't carry a lot of common sense,' Dr. John told him frankly. 'Matter of fact, Jason, I'd feel a lot easier about you if you could simmer down and start behaving yourself. Frankly, I'm not a bit happy about your E.C.G. today. Don't you *want* to get well?'

Jason turned a bitter gaze on him.

'Why should I?'

Dr. John made a little impatient gesture with his well-tended surgeon's hand, and his

22

brows drew together in a frown.

'Oh, come now, Jason,' he protested. 'You should be ashamed of a remark like that. Here we are, all of us, doing everything we possibly can to help you get well.'

'Which we both know I never will, with this heart condition and the arteries and all the rest of it.' Jason tucked the words in between Dr. John's protests.

Dr. John said, 'Well, I grant you that you may never be able to drive yourself the way you've been accustomed to doing; but you've got years ahead of you.'

'Years for what? To come apart at the seams and sit in the sun and become senile?'

Dr. John regarded him with frank disfavor.

'That, of course, is up to you,' he said curtly. 'There are many things a man in your condition can do if he really wants to.'

'Name one,' demanded Jason, and was more nearly his old, grouchy, unpleasant self than at any time during the afternoon. 'Run around through the hospital, like that Settles woman, and read aloud to the patients?'

Dr. John said firmly, 'We wouldn't allow you to do that even if you wanted to.'

'Well, don't worry about it. It's about the last thing in the world, I'd want to do,' Jason assured him.

'And it's about the last thing in the world we would allow you to do,' Dr. John responded. 'But there are other things you can do, if you'll just behave yourself and let us get you well and out of the hospital and back in your own home.'

Jason's thin lip curled. 'Home!' His tone made an imprecation of the word.

'It's a very nice house, Jason. And it has a nice lawn and shrubbery and flowers, and we have a man who wants very much to live with you and take care of you.'

'A male nurse?' Jason's tone told how little that idea appealed to him.

'No, a retired man whose pension is too small to allow him to buy a place of his own. He's strong and husky and loves outdoor work, and we've checked on his ability. He's a good cook, an excellent houseman—'

'Then why is he out of a job, if he's so good?'

'He isn't. He works here at the hospital. But I have talked to him about taking care of you as soon as you are able to leave the hospital, and he wants very much to do it.'

'How soon will I be leaving here?'

'That's up to you,' Dr. John told him. 'Behave yourself, get rid of this evil temper, stop getting excited and yelling at people and poisoning yourself with hatred and the lust for vengeance, and you ought to be out of here in two or three weeks.'

Jason studied him curiously for a long moment and then asked dryly, 'And if I don't do as I'm told?'

24

Dr. John stood up and spread his hands in a little gesture that expressed complete futility.

'You know the answer to that as well as I do,' he said flatly. 'We're doing all we can, but you have to co-operate with us, Jason.'

'Thanks,' said Jason dryly, 'for nothing.'

Dr. John looked down at him, exasperated. Then he lifted his plump shoulders in a slight shrug and turned toward the door.

'Have it your way, Jason!' he said shortly. He walked out of the room, and the door swung shut behind him.

Jason lay for a long time, completely quiet, deep in thought.

His supper tray was brought by a timid little aide who scurried out of the room afterwards as fast as she could. But Jason was too engrossed in his thoughts even to be aware of her.

He ate the supper absent-mindedly, scarcely aware of what it was. It could have been sawdust and ashes for all the taste it had to him, and he merely ate it automatically because it was expected of him and easier to eat it than to explain why he hadn't when they came back for the tray.

CHAPTER THREE

Martia had just settled herself with her breakfast tray in the cafeteria when her friend, Ellen Manning, on duty at night in the emergency ward, came toward her, carrying the tray that held the meal that was her supper.

'Too bad you missed all the excitement last night,' she remarked as she settled herself and dug hungrily into her food.

Martia's eyebrows went up, and she laughed.

'Excitement? At Sunset Acres? Pal, you're out of your mind!' she mocked lightly.

Ellen grinned at her.

'Ever hear of a man named Francis Malloy Conrad?' she asked.

Martia was startled.

'One of the richest and most feared men in the country. Who hasn't?' she gasped. 'Don't tell me he has moved to Sunset Acres!'

'Not him. His daughter. The one named Beatrice May Conrad, but who is known by all the gossip columnists and young rebels as Beatsie!' Ellen was pleased by the effect of her announcement.

Martia's eyes were wide and astonished.

'And what, in heaven's name, is Beatsie Conrad doing here?' she demanded.

26

'Getting herself patched up and glued together after as spectacular a car smash-up as anybody would expect to see during Memorial Day races at Indianapolis,' Ellen answered. 'Evidently nobody ever told her that the roads through Sunset Acres weren't built for hundred-mile-an-hour travel. She lost control on a curve just below the hospital and—*boom*!'

'Was she badly hurt?'

Ellen grinned sardonically.

'Well, she didn't exactly walk away from it. And the car was completely demolished. A very expensive foreign sports car. It's just junk now. But then what else would you expect Beatsie Conrad to be driving? The young man wasn't badly hurt, which is a pity, I'm afraid. He's strictly a nothing, a beatnik who obviously feels shaving and bathing and such are for "squares," not for young rebels.'

'The Conrad girl with a man like that!' Martia marveled.

'Oh, well, from what I've read about her, she rebels against everything and everybody that even hints at discipline or even ordinary decency.' Ellen shrugged. 'Dr. John and Dr. Hayden worked for hours patching her up. You name a broken bone; she's got it. Her face was badly cut, but Dr. John doesn't think there will be any scars. She'll walk again, he thinks, though there was some damage to the spine; and the broken leg should mend without too much trouble. She was a mess when they brought her in.'

Martia was genuinely compassionate. 'The poor girl!'

Ellen nodded. 'Oh, sure, I'm sorry for her, too. But a gal who drives a car a hundred miles an hour over roads that aren't really built for such speed can't expect to escape a smash-up.'

She stood up, grinned at Martia and said cheerfully, 'Well, she's all yours now. Room 329. One of the four private rooms we have here. She was so badly banged up that it was unthinkable to put her in a ward. See you later.'

She walked away, and Martia poured a second cup of coffee from the container before her and went a little pink as she saw Peter Hayden coming toward her with his tray.

He looked down at her, smiling, a caressing light in his eyes, and asked politely, 'Mind if I sit here?'

'Of course not, Doctor.' She smiled at him and hoped he was not aware of her heightened color as she said quickly, 'Ellen was telling me about the car crash last night. It must have given you and Dr. John a very busy evening. Will the girl recover?'

'Oh, I think so, and so does Dr. John,' Peter answered. 'Of course, if she had been one of our residents, she'd have been dead when she was pulled out of the wreckage. But she's young, strong and healthy. I feel sure she will make it.'

'And the young man with her?' asked Martia.

Peter chuckled. 'I think what shocked and hurt him most of all was being given a good hot bath and a lot of scrubbing. Two of the orderlies took him over as soon as we realized his injuries were not serious; you should have heard him howl. Seemed to think good hot soapy water would poison him.'

'I can't imagine why she should have been so badly hurt and he escaped so easily,' Martia puzzled.

'Oh, I think it must have been because she was driving,' Peter answered casually, although his eyes were warm and caressing. 'He was thrown clear. He may have seen the crash coming and been able to swing the door open on his side. Apart from some bruises and a contusion here and there, he escaped without a bit of damage, except for the bath and the shave, which just about wrecked him. He was quite proud of his beard; complained it would take him months to grow another one as handsome!'

Martia laughed at his tone and at his grimace. And then, because the warmth in his eyes was bringing deepened color to her cheeks, she pushed back her chair and stood up.

'I have to get busy, Doctor,' she told him politely. 'I'll see you on morning rounds.'

'You will indeed,' he agreed.

Martia went into the room that bore the number 329 in bold letters on its door, checked the condition of the patient and looked down at her with deep compassion.

The girl lay flat on her back, because of the cast that enveloped her from under the arms to the hips. One arm was in traction, the other heavily bandaged. Her face was half-hidden beneath bandages, and only her closed eyes and her mouth were visible. Golden hair the color of corn silk was spread on the pillow, a sharp patch of it cut away above the left temple, indicating that there had been some small surgery necessary on the head at that point.

The girl was under sedation, and her breath came slowly in hollow gasps. But the pulse was as strong as Martia had dared to hope, and she went on about her busy round somewhat encouraged about the girl.

It was three days before the girl became conscious of her surroundings and an aide summoned Martia to her room.

The girl's eyes were open, and they were deep, dark blue pools of bewilderment, as she managed the classic question, 'Where am I?'

Martia, her fingers on the girl's pulse, smiled down at her warmly.

'In a hospital, Miss Conrad,' she answered gently.

'Well, cripes, I knew that!' The girl's voice was curt and touched with an arrogance that Martia told herself she should have expected from such a girl. 'But what kind of a hospital, and where, and what am I doing here?'

'We sincerely hope you are getting well, Miss Conrad,' Martia assured her. 'We're doing all that we can to bring that about. You're in a hospital at a place called Sunset Acres, a retirement village for geriatrics.'

Puzzled, the girl repeated, 'Geriatrics?' And then, with a little gasp, she cried out, 'You mean a dump for old people? What am *I* doing here?'

'You smashed your car practically in front of the place, and you were so badly hurt that you were brought in here and put to bed,' Martia explained gently. 'We're trying to make you as comfortable as we can.'

The girl's voice crashed across hers, and the blue eyes were pools of alarm.

'And Jutsie?' she asked.

'Jutsie?' Martia repeated.

The girl's uninjured hand made a little gesture of disgust.

'He was with me in the car. We were eloping,' she explained as though no further explanation were necessary.

31

'Oh, yes, the young man traveling with you,' Martia answered, and decided that the most merciful thing was to deliver the blow at once. 'I'm afraid he's gone.'

The girl jerked, and Martia heard her gasp. 'You mean he's dead?'

'Oh, my goodness, no!' Martia answered swiftly. 'He wasn't badly hurt at all. He's left the hospital.'

'I suppose he's waiting for me in this crazy village,' said the girl.

'I'm afraid not,' Martia answered. 'Last we heard, he was heading for California. Said he wanted to get there in time for the grunion run.'

The blue eyes were wide with shock and incredulity.

'You mean he walked out on me?' she gasped. 'Why, that dirty, stinkin' louse!'

Martia said quickly, 'Now, Miss Conrad, that's not very ladylike.'

'Ladylike?' Beatsie's voice was harsh and rasping. 'In the gang I travel with, "lady" is an insult.'

'One not too often used, I'm sure.' Martia could not stop herself from saying it, but the girl's thoughts were evidently elsewhere.

'Does my father know about all this? What happened? Where am I?' she asked at last, and it seemed to Martia that there was a faintly wistful note in her voice.

'Of course,' Martia told her gently. 'We

wired him as soon as we identified you.'

'And I suppose he is here,' said Beatsie as if there could not possibly be any doubt of that.

'I'm afraid not,' Martia had to tell her. 'But he sent his legal representative.'

'Old Turkey-Wattles, I suppose,' Beatsie sneered. 'I hope you clapped him into a cell somewhere. A home for geriatrics is exactly where the old dodo belongs.'

'I believe it was a Mr. Hunnicutt who came,' Martia told her.

'Old Honey-Bee?' the girl seemed not only startled but outraged. 'Why, he's a nothing! Strictly a leg man for Dad's gang of legal eagles. Honey-Bee is never allowed to do anything but the most menial jobs—and Dad sent him here when he knew I was smashed up! I'd like to speak to old H.B.! I'd like to tell him a few things he can pass on to my unesteemed parent! I wouldn't dare write them to Dad unless I had some asbestos stationery.'

'Mr. Hunnicutt has gone,' Martia said quietly. 'He only stayed overnight and then left. But he opened a checking account for you at the local bank. And your friend Jutsie went with him as far as Sarasota.'

The girl lay very still for a long moment.

'So old Honey-Bee paid Jutsie off, and the louse took the payoff and blasted off!' the girl said just above her breath, and her eyes were slightly sick.

Martia said gently, 'Were you very much in love with him?'

Contempt vanquished the sick pain in Beatsie's eyes, and her soft mouth beneath the bandages was twisted bitterly.

'In love with him? What are you—a square? Don't tell me you are fool enough to believe in all that nonsense about love and marriage and happiness and all that drivel!' she sneered.

Martia smiled.

'I'm afraid I'm just that foolish,' she admitted entirely without shame.

'Well, how can you be, with the world rapidly going to Hades in a basket?'

'To begin with, I don't for a moment believe the world is going to Hades in a basket, as you so prettily express it. And I happen to know that love is just about the most important thing in all the world.'

The girl's eyes were brimming with contempt when she sneered, 'More even than the bomb?'

'Much more,' Martia insisted. 'But, of course, you're much too young to realize that, since you were eloping with a man you admit you do not love.'

'Love? Phooey! Pap for squares and elderly people like you,' snapped Beatsie.

'But very nice pap.' Martia forbore to argue with her and went on, 'There's a young man who wants very much to talk to you. He's been here every day since the accident, and I promised him he could have five minutes with you when you were able to talk. Shall I bring him in?'

'Who is he and what does he want?'

'He's Kirby Clarke, who owns and operates the local weekly newspaper and is local correspondent for some of the big city newspapers. And he wants to do a story about you, an interview to follow up the stories he sent out about the accident.'

Beatsie's interest deepened the color of her eyes, and a wicked gleam dawned there.

'Well, bring him in,' she ordered. 'I'll give him a story that will knock his teeth out!'

As Martia turned toward the door, she asked, 'What's he like—this newspaper guy?'

'Oh, he's very nice,' Martia assured her. 'You'll like him. Everybody does!'

'Huh!' Beatsie's tone frankly doubted that. 'Another square, like you, I suppose. Well, bring him on in. If he's in the newspaper business, I have a story to give him that ought to send him way out.'

Martia hesitated for a moment, and then she walked out into the corridor, where a tall, lanky young man waited, his red hair an untidy thatch, his brown eyes taking in with lively appreciation the pretty little aides that were elaborately unconscious of him, as they paraded the corridor on their duties.

As Martia emerged from room 329, he came eagerly to meet her, his eyes eager as Martia said briskly, 'Five minutes, Kirby. No more.'

'Yessum,' said Kirby happily. 'I'm quite sure I can get all the dope I want from her in five minutes. Or I can come back again later.'

Martia ushered him into the room and said pleasantly,'Miss Conrad, this is Kirby Clarke.'

Beatsie's blue eyes regarded him appraisingly.

'So you're a newspaper lad,' she commented. 'Where's your tape recorder?'

Kirby looked slightly disturbed.

'Tape recorder, Miss Conrad?' he repeated.

'I thought they were standard equipment for an interview,' she said, and her voice was curt.

'Oh, I'm just a country boy, Miss Conrad. We have very little use for such fancy city doodads as tape recorders. I still make notes in my little black book and then type the story out after I get back to the office.'

'Then how can I be sure you won't misquote me?' she snapped.

Kirby's eyes were quizzical, but his voice was properly polite as he said, 'I'm afraid you'll have to trust me, Miss Conrad. I rarely misquote!'

And before she could manage an answer to that, he had drawn out a battered notebook, poised a pen above a clean page and added, 'One thing there is no danger of my misquoting, Miss Conrad. That's the fact that when you start out to smash a car, the 500-milers at Indianapolis on Memorial Day couldn't do a better job.'

'I've always prided myself on doing thoroughly whatever I do,' she snapped.

Kirby nodded. 'Now do you mind telling me, Miss Conrad, what you were doing? I mean, where were you headed when the accident happened?'

'Miami, of course; where else?'

'Then why the Gulf coast instead of the East Coast?'

'To avoid my father's hired thugs, who were stationed along the main highway over there determined to stop us,' she answered. 'I knew they would never think of looking for us over here. So we followed some sideroads and a detour or two—and here I am.'

Kirby nodded thoughtfully, his eyes taking in the various indications of her injuries.

'Yes, ma'am, and so you are,' he agreed, and added, 'your father, I take it, objected to your elopement with this Jutsie guy?'

'Well, of course,' she snapped as though she found the question almost too silly to answer. 'Why else would I have done it, if not to give him a bad time?'

Kirby and Martia both looked mildly startled, and Kirby asked, 'Your father is Francis Malloy Conrad, the famous philanthropist?'

'Ha!' Beatsie's tone was a mixture of disgust and contempt. 'You mean he contributes millions to organizations, colleges, hospitals and any places he feels sure will give him the most favorable publicity. But most of all he does it to keep from giving the money to the government in taxes. He hates the government almost as much as he hates me. And that's puh-lenty, you'd better believe me. But much as he hates me, I hate him even more! He's strictly a no-good in my book, and I was eloping with Jutsie in the hope of getting myself lost in his gang so that people would forget I'm Beatsie Conrad.'

Her blue eyes sharpened as she saw that his pen had not touched the clean page of the notebook, and she cried out sharply, 'Are you getting all this down?'

'Of course not, did you really think I would? Ever hear about the laws of libel, Miss Conrad?' Kirby asked her politely.

'Don't call me Miss Conrad! I loathe the name! And the minute I get out of here and can find an unmarried man, I'm going to marry him just to get my name changed, even if I have to divorce him ten minutes later!' Then a sudden idea hit her and she

38

demanded sternly of Kirby, 'Are *you* married?'

Kirby blinked and said hurriedly, 'No, ma'am. And no intention of being, either, for a long, long time.'

'Not even if I offer you a great deal of money just to marry me long enough for me to use your name?' she persisted.

Kirby stared at her, his dandy brows going up. Then he turned to Martia and said curiously, 'She's got to be in delirium or something. She can't be for real.'

'Oh, shut up!' Beatsie ordered him grimly. 'I made you a business proposition. Let's not make a production of it. I just wanted to use your name, that's all.'

Kirby grinned at her infuriatingly.

'The good old married-in-name-only gambit? Sorry, ma'am—I'm waiting until I fall in love.'

'*Will* you stop calling me "ma'am"? It makes me feel as old as some of these creeps I see tottering past the door when it's left open,' snapped Beatsie furiously.

Kirby lifted quizzical eyes to Martia, who had come forward unobtrusively and put her fingers on the girl's pulse. Beatsie jerked her wrist away and snapped, 'Oh, for Pete's sake, leave me alone!'

'Sassy little piece, isn't she?' Kirby said blandly.

'If you don't want me to tell you about my

father and why we hate each other—' she began furiously.

'Oh, but I do, Miss Conrad, I do!' Kirby assured her. 'Oh, not because I have any idea of making a story out of it, but because you seem to be so anxious to tell it. Proceed, lady.'

'Careful, Kirby,' Martia warned him. 'She feels the word is an insult.'

Kirby nodded. 'That's understandable,' he said, and added to Beatsie, 'so let's have it, ma'am. Why does your father hate you? Which I don't for a moment believe.'

'Well, you'd better,' Beatsie told him sulkily. 'The only person in the world my old man ever loved was my mother. She died when I was born, and he has never forgiven me for murdering her.'

'Why, Beatsie, that's ridiculous!' Martia protested.

The deep blue eyes flung her a glance of the utmost bitterness.

'From the day I was born, he never came near me. I was turned over to nurses and then to a governess, and I was always warned never to be anywhere near him when he came home. Once when I was about seven, and very lonely for something or someone to love, I hid behind the stairs. And when he came home from the office, I ran out and flung myself against him and begged him to love me. He looked down at me as though I

40

had been something that had crawled out from under a rock after a heavy rain-storm and yelled for someone to take me back to the nursery.'

The dark blue eyes now were filled with tears, and Martia and Kirby exchanged compassionate glances. Before either of them could speak, the tired, low voice went on:

'From that moment on, I hated him. I grew up hating him. And whenever I could find something to do that I knew would make him livid with rage, I couldn't wait to do it!' The tears were gone now, and the soft mouth was a thin, twisted line of bitterness. 'And I was pretty imaginative. Of course, it wasn't too hard to do things that made him angry, and of course each time we hated each other a little more. But if Jutsie and I had finished our elopement as we planned, *that* would have put the tin hat on! He would never have forgiven me—and that's what I wanted. Because I'll never forgive *him*, not if I live long enough to be a resident in good standing of this pad!'

'Beatsie,' said Martia gently, her eyes deeply compassionate, 'you must realize, my dear, that hating him injures you. It doesn't hurt him.'

'You are so right!' Beatsie almost spat the words out. 'The only thing I can do to hurt him is to get his precious name in the papers in a scandalous way. And I pride myself I've

41

done a real neat job of that.'

Martia and Kirby exchanged glances, and Martia said briskly, 'I'm afraid you'll have to leave now, Kirby. She's getting wrought up, and that's not good for her.'

'Sure,' Kirby agreed, and thrust his notebook in his pocket, the clean fresh page unsullied by so much as a word.

'You're not going to do a story about me and Jutsie?' Beatsie objected. 'You're not going to expose my old man as the hypocrite he is, a real stinker?'

'I am not,' Kirby assured her firmly. 'I have due respect for libel laws, even if you don't.'

'You filthy coward!' Beatsie flung at him. 'You're scared of him!'

Kirby looked back at her, his brows raised.

'Well, of course I'm scared of him,' he admitted without shame, 'like a mouse is scared of a jungle cat.'

The door closed behind him and Martia, but they took with them the memory of the girl's eyes, almost black with helpless fury.

'That poor kid!' said Kirby, when they stood outside the closed door. 'Her father must really be the stinker of all time!'

'Or else they have never bothered to try to understand each other,' Martia suggested without too much conviction.

Kirby looked down at her, and now the brown eyes were warm and tender, and his smile was a caress.

'Martia, Martia, my love,' he mocked her, a hand on her shoulder, 'I wonder if ever in this cockeyed world you could find somebody for whom you didn't have a kind word.'

Martia smiled ruefully.

'Well, as a nurse, I was taught from the very beginning to give the patient the benefit of the doubt,' she admitted.

There was a brisk footfall along the corridor, and she turned swiftly to see Peter Hayden approaching them. She stepped back from Kirby's hand as Peter said crisply, 'If you're quite free, Miss Stapleton, I'd like to check on the Conrad girl.'

'Of course, Doctor,' Martia said politely.

'Hi, Peter,' Kirby said lightly. And to Martia, 'I'll see you around, Martia.'

Martia smiled at him as he gave her a little friendly wave and walked away.

Peter looked down at Martia, scowling.

'I hope you haven't been allowing him to interview the Conrad girl.' His tone was accusing.

Startled, Martia said, 'Why, Dr. John gave him permission.'

'Really? The Conrad girl is my patient, and I would certainly never have granted such permission,' said Peter, an edge in his tone, as he thrust the door open and walked ahead of her into the room.

Beatsie lay with her eyes closed, and there was the stain of tears around them. But as Peter took her wrist, her eyes opened and she looked up at him.

'Well, what do you want?' she snapped at him ungraciously.

'Just to check your condition.' He smiled down at her. 'I'm your doctor.'

'So? I don't remember seeing you before.'

'Well, this is the first time you've been in a condition to recognize anybody, Miss Conrad,' Peter assured her as he made a swift but complete examination, while Martia stood on the other side of the bed, ready to be an extra pair of hands for him should he need them.

Beatsie watched him curiously as he completed the examination and asked, 'What's your name? Forgive me if I've forgotten.'

'You probably haven't even heard it.' Peter again smiled at her. 'I'm Dr. Hayden.'

'Dr. Hayden!' she mused thoughtfully. And then, so suddenly that Martia caught her breath, Beatsie demanded, 'Are you married, Doctor?'

Startled, Peter said, 'Why, no.'

'That's good,' said Beatsie happily. 'Stick around, Doc. I may have an interesting proposition to make to you as soon as I'm able to leave here. How soon will that be?'

Peter studied her, a twinkle in his dark

eyes, a faint smile tugging at the corners of his mouth.

'Several weeks, I'm afraid. But we'll try very hard to make you comfortable.'

'Oh, I'm not worrying about that,' Beatsie assured him happily. And then she added anxiously, 'You're not against marriage, are you, Doc?'

Peter laughed. 'Of course not.'

'That's good.' Beatsie beamed at him. 'I think all doctors *should* be married, don't you?'

'Undoubtedly.' His dark eyes were brimming with amusement.

'But you've just not gotten around to it yet. Is that it?' demanded Beatsie, a trace of anxiety in her voice.

'Well, let's just say I'm working on it,' he answered with a slight laugh as he turned toward the door.

'Well, don't work too hard on it,' Beatsie ordered firmly. 'Not, at least, until you hear my proposition. I think you'll be interested!'

Outside in the corridor, Peter looked down at Martia, his brow furrowed in a slight frown, and asked, 'Now what was that all about?'

Martia smiled up at him. 'Beatsie is campaigning for a husband,' she told him. 'She wants to drop the name of Conrad as soon as she can. She made Kirby the offer and scared him half to death.'

Peter's amusement fled, and the furrow deepened.

'Well, of course, since Kirby has other plans.'

'Oh, has he? I hadn't heard.'

'Really? I'd think you'd be the first to hear.'

Martia stared at him, bewildered.

'I'm afraid I don't know what you're talking about, Doctor,' she replied.

'Don't you? That's a bit hard to believe,' said Peter, and walked away from her, leaving her standing there, looking after him with a puzzled frown on her lovely face.

Now what, she asked herself as she went about her busy round during the day, did he mean by that?

CHAPTER FOUR

Martia came down the wide aisle between the double row of beds in the morning, her quick eyes taking in everything even as she smiled a pleasant good morning at the patients.

At the end of the ward, curtains had been drawn around a bed, and Martia stepped inside the small cubbyhole that the curtains made.

The woman who lay there was a long,

gaunt shape that barely lifted the covers, and her eyes were heavily bandaged. Beside her head on the pillow there was a big, heavy sandbag wrapped in a clean, soft towel, to prevent the woman from turning her head.

'Good morning, Mrs. Jackson,' said Martia pleasantly. 'I've come to change the dressing on your eyes.'

'Who are you?' asked the woman, her voice faint and tired.

'I'm Martia Stapleton, Mrs. Jackson. Your nurse,' Martia told her gently as she began removing the tape that held the bandages in place.

'Oh, yessum.' The voice was tired, and the woman flinched as Martia removed the tape, examined one eye and put drops into it.

'Are you very uncomfortable, Mrs. Jackson?' asked Martia as she taped up the eye and began on the other one. 'It's too bad you had both cataracts removed at the same time. But you're doing just fine, Mrs. Jackson! And won't it be wonderful to be able to read your own mail again?'

The woman sighed. 'I don't get any mail,' she answered matter of factly. 'There's nobody to write to me. My husband was all the family I had. Since he died, I just haven't gotten around to meeting folks who would write to me.'

'I'm sorry,' Martia said gently.

'Oh, I'm used to it now,' the woman

answered. 'My husband's been dead four years, and I knew I had to adjust to living by myself, doing what had to be done and trying not to worry about the things I couldn't do any more.'

'That's very brave of you, Mrs. Jackson.'

'Brave?' The woman's hand, whose roughness showed she was no stranger to hard work, made a slight gesture. 'Somebody said once, "How brave is desperation?" I've always remembered that.'

'I still think you are very brave,' Martia told her. 'Not many people have the courage to have both eyes operated on at the same time.'

Something that faintly resembled a chuckle came from the woman's scrawny, sun-tanned throat.

'Well, they was both so bad the doctor couldn't make up his mind which one ought to be tended to first, and I told him just to go ahead and get 'em both fixed up at the same time.'

Martia had finished the dressings and stood beside the bed for a moment. The woman put out her hand with a fumbling gesture, and Martia grasped it in both her own with a warm, comforting pressure.

'When the folks at the church realized I was pretty near blind, the preacher come to see me and said I ought to sell the farm and buy me a place in a retirement village,' she

48

said slowly. 'And he helped me find this one. I reckon I didn't make no mistake. Folks are awful kind here, and I've got me a right nice little apartment. Soon's I get well, I know I'm going to have a sight of fun fixing it all up real pretty.'

'Of course you will, Mrs. Jackson,' Martia soothed her gently. 'And we like to think you made no mistake in coming to Sunset Acres.'

'Sunset Acres!' Mrs. Jackson seemed to turn the words over on her tongue as though they had a pleasant taste. 'I think maybe it was that name that settled me in my mind to come here. George and me used to like to watch the sunset. Our house faced the west, and we'd get us good comfortable chairs and set down on the porch after supper and watch the sun go down. It was mighty pretty.'

'I know it must have been,' Martia assured her. 'Down here, you will like watching the sun set over the Gulf, and the afterglow that makes all the trees and shrubbery and the flowers look as if somebody had painted them with a golden brush.'

The woman's face was touched with a shy but eager smile beneath the bandages.

'You make it sound awful pretty,' she said happily. 'I couldn't see much more than my hand in front of my face when I first got here, but I know when I get my new eyes I'm going to find a beautiful new world.'

'I'm sure you will, Mrs. Jackson,' said Martia.

'I'm hindering you,' the woman said hastily. 'I know you must be busier than a bee in a tar-bucket.'

'I'm never too busy to listen to you, Mrs. Jackson.'

'Would you maybe do me a real big favor?' the woman asked hesitantly.

'Of course, Mrs. Jackson, if I can.'

'Would you call me Miss Sairy, instead of Mrs. Jackson?' The woman's words came in an abashed rush. 'Seems to me like I can't never get used to being called Mrs. Jackson. Folks back home always called me Miss Sairy, and it seemed like it was kinda more friendly like.'

'Then of course I'll call you Miss Sairy,' Martia told her warmly.

'I'm thanking you, Miss Stapleton,' said the woman with old-fashioned courtesy. 'You're awful kind.'

'I'm glad you think so,' Martia assured her. 'Is there anything I can get you to make you more comfortable?'

'Well, no, I reckon not, thank you. I'm real comfortable.'

'Good! Then if you think of anything you'd like, you just push that little button there on the rack beside you. Can you reach it?'

Martia took the work-scarred hand gently

in her own and guided it to the small cord that lay beneath the towel-wrapped sandbag.

'Oh, yessum, I can reach it easy,' the woman answered happily. 'I don't reckon I'll need it, though. Folks here seem to be mighty busy doing everything they can for us.'

'That's what we are here for,' Martia told her, and went away.

It would be hard, she told herself as she went her rounds, to find a place where there was more variety among people than in a hospital, especially one like this where all the patients were in their sixties or beyond. Some of them were querulous, fault-finding, difficult; some were like Mrs. Jackson, so humble and so appreciative of the slightest gesture of friendliness and comfort that they made a nurse want to create miracles of healing that were beyond even the most skilled doctor's efforts.

And then, she reminded herself ruefully as she made up the medication trays, there are the Jason Weathersbees and the Beatsie Conrads whom nothing and nobody can please.

It was several days later that Martia encountered Miss Laura Settles in the corridor. Miss Laura was beaming. Her eyes were alight, and as she faced Martia she shifted the package of books and magazines in her arms.

'Martia, the loveliest thing has happened,' she related happily. 'I stopped in the ward, and there was a new patient, Mrs. Marshall, and it turns out we have mutual friends and mutual interests! She was active in PTA work back in Atlanta, and while we never met, we do know a lot of the same people.'

'That's lovely, Miss Laura. I'm so glad,' Martia told her sincerely.

Miss Laura laughed. 'We had a lovely time tearing the school board to bits. Verbally, of course.'

'I can't believe that, Miss Laura,' Martia protested with a smile. 'You're much too kind to want to tear anyone to bits.'

'Well, there is always considerable friction between the school board and the teachers; and sometimes between the teachers and the PTA. It seems we can't understand each other's problems. And then there are the children, caught in the middle and not really knowing or understanding what's going on.'

She sighed, shifted the load of books and magazines and added happily, 'As soon as Mrs. Marshall is up and around again, she and I plan to see a lot of each other.'

'I'm so glad,' Martia told her, and on a sudden impulse added, 'We have another new patient, Miss Laura, that I don't think you've met: a teen-ager.'

'At Sunset Acres?' Miss Laura marveled, and then went on, 'Oh, yes, I believe I read about her. The Conrad girl, isn't she? Daughter of a very wealthy man whose car cracked up here.'

Martia nodded. 'That's the one. I wondered if you'd like to meet her.'

'Well of course. Perhaps I can cheer the child up a bit. Unless, of course, she has her father with her.'

'It seems that he couldn't get away from his business, and I don't think she knows anyone close enough to visit her. I'm sure you could cheer her up. She must be very lonely.'

'The poor child!' Miss Laura followed Martia into room 329. Beatsie turned her head, and dark blue eyes, sick with misery, glanced at them.

'Well, what do you want?' she snapped.

'I've brought you a visitor, Beatsie,' said Martia gently. 'This is Miss Laura Settles. Miss Laura, this is Beatsie Conrad.'

Miss Laura smiled warmly. 'What an odd name, Beatsie.'

'It's a nickname, of course,' Beatsie told her ungraciously. 'How'd *you* like to be called Beatrice May?'

Miss Laura smiled and seated herself, depositing the books and magazines on the small table beside her.

'Parents do have a way of saddling their offspring with names that they grow up to hate, don't they?' she asked. 'I know some of

53

the boys and girls in my classes just hated their names, and many's the fight that has wound up with bloody noses and black eyes because somebody called somebody else by his real name.'

'You're a schoolteacher?' demanded Beatsie.

'I was,' Miss Laura replied. 'I'm retired now.'

'And you live here in this cockeyed place?'

'It's really a very lovely place, Beatsie, as you will find out when you are able to be up and around and really see it,' Miss Laura told her.

Thinking the visit was going much better than she had hoped, Martia slipped unobtrusively out of the room and came face to face with Dr. Peter Hayden.

'Oh, good morning, Doctor,' she greeted him in the approved manner of a well-trained nurse.

'Good morning, Nurse.' His manner was equally the approved one as he gestured toward 329. 'How is she this morning?'

'Oh, she's fine.' Martia held out the chart for him to scan. 'She has a visitor.'

Peter looked up swiftly, his brows drawn together.

'Clarke is back again? A persistent cuss, isn't he?' His voice barely missed being a growl.

Conscious of the slight warmth in her

cheeks that told her she was flushing, Martia answered quietly, 'No, it's Miss Laura Settles. I don't think Kirby will be back. Not to see her, anyway. She scared him off.'

'Really? That's quite a feat. I didn't think anybody could scare a newspaper man off a story he wanted to write.'

'The story she gave him was how much she and her father hated each other and what a—I believe "stinker" was the word she used—he was. Kirby knew no such story could be written,' Martia explained quietly. 'And then she suggested she would like the use of the Clarke name. By marrying him briefly—'

'Briefly?'

'She explained she only wanted the use of his name so she could scrap the Conrad name forever and disappear into the limbo of her beatnik friends,' Martia told him, and added, 'she's really a very mixed-up girl, and very confused. She is convinced her father hates her.'

'Too bad we don't have a psychiatric unit here,' Peter cut in curtly. 'But I dare say she can find a good one as soon as she is out of here.'

He turned away, hesitated and then turned back, scowling down at her.

'I don't suppose it would do any good at all for me to ask you to have dinner with me tonight.' His tone made it a statement rather than a question. 'That is, if you're sure Clarke can spare you for an evening.'

'Well, you might try,' she suggested coolly, now the woman rather than the nurse.

'Don't flirt with me, Martia!' His tone was a growl. He took a step closer to her, and his arms made an involuntary movement, before he caught himself and thrust his hands deep into the pockets of his white coat.

The color poured into Martia's face, and her eyes fell before his.

'Don't be ridiculous, Doctor,' she began.

'Peter,' he cut in.

'All right, then. Peter. I'm not flirting with you! I just said that I'd be glad to have dinner with you.'

His dark eyes were alight, and his handsome, sun-tanned face was warmed by an eager smile.

'Hey, that's great!' he said happily, and added anxiously, 'you don't have a date with Kirby Clarke?'

'Of course not!' she sputtered indignantly. 'Kirby and I are friends, but he's years younger than I am.'

'As if that made a difference. A couple of years—'

'It's much more than that. Kirby is twenty-five. And I'm twenty-eight.'

'Practically tottering on the brink,' he said gravely, but she was relieved to see that there was a twinkle in his eyes.

'Well, let's just say that I am old enough to realize how utterly silly it would be for me to become seriously interested in Kirby,' she insisted, 'or any man his age.'

Peter nodded gravely.

'I'm thirty-two,' he told her. 'Do I qualify?'

'For dinner. Yes, of course.'

'I didn't mean that, and you know it.' The twinkle had vanished now, and he was in deadly earnest. 'I meant qualify as a man in whom you could become seriously interested.'

Martia could not meet that steady, probing gaze and was relieved to be interrupted by an aide who said hurriedly, 'Excuse me, Miss Stapleton. Mr. Weathersbee is yelling—I mean he's insisting on seeing you, and he says to come "on the double."'

'Of course,' said Martia. She glanced at Peter and smiled disarmingly. 'I'm sorry, Doctor. Later, perhaps.'

'Later, of course,' said Peter, and Martia hurried away.

Jason Weathersbee scowled furiously at Martia and said, 'Well, here you are at last.'

Martia smiled sunnily at him.

'Did you want something, Mr. Weathersbee?' she asked.

'Would I have sent for you if I didn't?'

'Would you?'

'Certainly not,' he snapped, and added, 'where's that Settles woman? I haven't seen her in a week or two.'

'After the way you insulted her, did you think she'd be back?'

Jason had the grace to look mildly ashamed.

'Well, no, I suppose not,' he agreed unwillingly. 'But tell her I want to see her—right away.'

Martia smiled disarmingly. 'I'm afraid she's rather busy just now,' she answered.

His scowl deepened.

'Busy doing what? Reading "Get Well" cards to patients? You call that being busy?' he growled.

'Miss Laura does, and so do some of the patients.'

'Well, get her in here. I want to talk to her.'

'I'm afraid I'll have to promise her that if she comes in, you will apologize to her.'

His roar was like that of a wounded lion.

'Apologize?' he snorted when speech was once more possible. 'Me, Jason Weathersbee, apologize to that dowdy old frump? Are you out of your mind? Jason Weathersbee apologizes to nobody, miss!'

Martia said gently, 'That's too bad. Apologizing, saying you were wrong, sometimes is a great help.'

'You mean it keeps a person humble,' he

snorted. 'Well, I'm not humble. I never believed any of that guff about the meek inheriting the earth. The meek just get kicked around a little more, and the bold take over.'

'Like your nephews?' Martia suggested.

Jason dropped back on his pillow, and his lean jaw set hard.

'All right; go ahead and needle me,' he snapped, but now a good deal of the bite had gone out of his voice. 'I suppose I have it coming.'

'I'm afraid you do, Mr. Weathersbee,' Martia assured him, and though her tone was gentle it was also firm. 'If you'll promise to apologize to Miss Laura, I'll tell her you want to see her as soon as she is through with Beatsie Conrad.'

His scowl now was touched with bewilderment

'Beatsie? Now what kind of darn fool name is that for a resident of a retirement village?' he wanted to know.

'Oh, Beatsie isn't a resident. She's a patient. Her car smashed up practically at our doorstep. She's about twenty, I think, and I'm sure you can imagine how bored she is here.'

'If she's any more bored than I am, then I'm sorry for her,' Jason growled. 'But send the Settles woman along, will you?'

'Miss Laura will be here as soon as she is

free,' Martia assured him pleasantly. 'Is there anything else I can do to make you more comfortable?'

He made a little impatient gesture of dismissal and turned his head away.

'No, no, I've been "made more comfortable" all morning long. Now I'd like to be left alone—that is, until the Settles woman is free,' he growled.

Martia hesitated, and then she asked implacably, 'You will apologize to her, won't you? I can promise her that if she is reluctant to come in?'

'Oh, sure, sure, I'll apologize!' he snapped. 'Only get her in here.'

Martia nodded and walked out into the corridor, careful not to let him see the small smile that tugged at the corners of her pretty mouth.

She had very little time during the rest of the day to wonder why she had accepted Dr. Hayden's dinner invitation. She only knew that somehow, when he had asked her, she had said 'yes' without stopping to think. After all, why shouldn't she have dinner with him? She liked him enormously, and she had so persistently refused his invitations that it was beginning to grow a trifle embarrassing. And after all, what did merely having dinner with him involve? Nothing more than a pleasant evening, she assured herself firmly. And if the very firmness of her attempt to convince herself of that alarmed her slightly, she put the thought aside and refused to allow it to nibble at her mind.

Late in the afternoon, when she was in the nurses' station, preparing to go off duty, Dr. Hayden came striding down the corridor, looking very worried and scowling.

'Time for a cup of coffee?' he asked her brusquely.

Puzzled at his tone and his manner, she relegated her task to another nurse and walked with him to the cafeteria. He brought two cups of coffee and faced her across the table.

'I hope you know how much it breaks me up, Martia, to have to tell you I can't keep our dinner date after all.' He gave her the news in one fell swoop, and in spite of her effort to conceal it, Martia could not quite keep the disappointment from her eyes or her voice.

'That's quite all right, Doctor,' she began.

'Peter!' he insisted, and she smiled.

'You don't look a bit disappointed,' he scolded her.

'I am, of course, Doc—Peter,' she assured him hastily. 'But I'm sure you have a very good reason. It isn't just that you've changed your mind—or is it?'

'Don't be ridiculous!' he all but snorted at her. 'After I've tried for months to get a date with you, and finally succeeded, you surely aren't silly enough to think I didn't really want the date? You must know me better than that, Martia!'

'Well, there will be other times.'

'And other dates?'

'Of course, if you want them.'

He said barely above his breath, in a tone that made her heart give a small, startled leap, 'If I want them! You still don't have any idea, do you? Or is it that you don't want—' He broke off and spoke in his normal tone. 'Mr. McCallum is dying. He wants me with him. And of course, I want to help him all I can. He has always had a horror, he tells me, of dying alone. He has no family. So I could scarcely refuse to sit with him, could I?'

'I'd have despised you if you had,' Martia assured him warmly.

His look was warm and deep and ardent.

'That's my girl!' he said. And before she could manage an answer, he went on quietly, his eyes holding hers, 'Because you do know, don't you, that some day you are going to be my girl?'

Martia stammered faintly, 'Oh, please don't!'

His brows drew together in a slight scowl.

'Darling, are you afraid?' he asked very softly.

'Afraid?'

'Of falling in love again. Or is it that I

don't deserve such happiness?'

She could only look at him.

'I know, of course, what happened before,' he said very gently. 'But, my dearest dear, you can't live in the past. You're young, vital, and you mustn't be afraid to live and to love again.'

She could only murmur a wordless protest before Peter went on.

'I'm not going to crowd you, darling, or try to rush you,' he told her. 'It's just that I want you to know how I feel and that with all that is alive in me, I'm hoping that some day you will feel the same way about me. And when you do, my dearest, we'll have the world on a string!'

He stood up, smiling warmly down at her.

'We'll leave it at that for now, darling,' he told her. 'I just wanted you to know how it is with me, how it will always be.'

For a moment that seemed to her endless, he stood looking down at her, and his eyes on her tremulous mouth were so ardent that she felt as though he had kissed her. Then he walked away and left her sitting there, wide-eyed and shaken to the depths of her being.

There was a wild panic in her heart that warned her to run as fast as she could. But something even stronger than the panic warned her that no matter where she ran or how fast, she would not escape.

CHAPTER FIVE

Martia was still mildly uneasy when she came on duty the next morning. But Peter's manner was as casual, as matter of fact as though there had never been any scene over two cups of coffee in the cafeteria. If he had meant what he had said, he seemed to have no intention of following it up. And Martia was feminine enough to be a little provoked at his matter-of-fact behavior. Now and then, during their busy morning, she thought she caught a slight twinkle in his eyes, as though he sensed her thoughts, and that did nothing to alleviate her uneasiness.

With the recuperative powers of the young, Beatsie was making an excellent recovery. But her disposition was not improving at all, and Martia was more than a little annoyed with her.

She came into room 329 one morning after the usual rounds and stood looking down at Beatsie. Some of the bandages had been removed from her face and replaced by bits of adhesive that made it possible to see her sulky expression.

'Well, what do you want?' she snapped ungraciously.

'Just to say good morning and ask how you're feeling!' Martia's tone was quite professional.

'How do you think I'm feeling, sealed up in cement and with my arm up over my head and aching in muscles I didn't even know I had.'

'I'm sorry.' Martia smiled. 'Would you like a sedative?'

'No, I wouldn't like a sedative.' Beatsie mimicked her voice. 'All I'd like is to get out of this mausoleum.'

'I'm sorry you find us so unpleasant.'

'Oh, for Pete's sake, stop being so sweet and gentle,' Beatsie snapped. 'It's like walking in maple syrup. Everybody's so sweet; nobody wants to argue or fight. It's all so sugary and friendly that it turns my stomach!'

Martia laughed. 'Well, if it's an argument you want, suppose I telephone Kirby Clarke?'

Beatsie's eyes grew less sullen.

'You mean that newspaper guy that didn't know a good story when one crawled up into his lap and bit him?' she asked, and there was a trace of eagerness in her voice.

'The one who knew so much about libel and slander laws that he saw no reason he should be wiped out with one fell swoop of your father's little finger,' Martia corrected her.

Beatsie said unwillingly, yet with the faintest possible trace of pride in her voice,

'Well, that's Daddy-o. He hits hard, and his arm is just about perfect.'

'And Kirby is a small town newspaperman who would be destroyed without a moment's hesitation by your Daddy-o.'

'He would, at that!'

She was silent for a moment, and then she grinned a small, impish grin.

'Get the Kirby gent over here!' she ordered. 'I feel like a good old-fashioned knock-down and drag-out fight with somebody less than a hundred years old. And he's the only one I know who has the time for a fight.'

'Well, I'm not sure that Kirby has that much time. The paper goes to press Thursday,' Martia pointed out.

'Call him anyway and tell him I want to see him,' Beatsie repeated her order.

'Yes, ma'am,' Martia mocked her, and left the room.

Kirby's voice was curt as he answered the phone.

'Well, what is it?' he snapped instead of the conventional 'Hello.'

'I'm passing along an order, Kirby,' Martia told him.

'I hope it's one that has a cash value.' Kirby's tone had altered as he recognized her voice. 'The monthly bank statements are just in, and they don't make very gladsome reading.'

Martia chuckled. 'I'm not sure this one has any cash value, Kirby,' she admitted. 'Miss Conrad craves to have a fight with you.'

'She does? What have I done to the gal now?' Kirby's tone was undisturbed, even slightly amused.

'It's not what you have done; it's what she hopes you will do,' Martia told him. 'She's a bit bored by all the other patients, which is understandable, of course; and she's more than a bit bored by her physical condition, which is also understandable. So she wants a fight with somebody; an argument; a flaming row. And of course we here are too well trained to argue with a patient.'

'Which I've always considered a downright shame,' Kirby answered firmly. 'Well, I can't make it right away. After all, I am a working man, which is something the poor kid never thought of. But I'll get over when I can.'

'Thanks, Kirby. I'll tell her,' Martia answered, and turned away from the phone.

Miss Laura was coming down the corridor, and Martia smiled at her.

'Oh, Martia, I can't tell you how glad I am that you sent me in to see Mr. Weathersbee again,' Miss Laura fluted happily. 'He's really a grand person!'

Martia stared at her in frank amazement.

'Mr. Weathersbee?' she repeated, astounded. 'Are we talking about the same man?'

Miss Laura laughed girlishly and shifted her armful of papers and magazines.

'Oh, I know he can be very difficult when he wants to be,' she admitted. 'But after all, he's been through an awful lot and he is a very sick man. Most of all, Martia, he's so terribly lonely.'

'Of course he is,' Martia answered. 'And I'm very glad he is behaving himself. I know he must enjoy your visits.'

A faint trace of pink showed in Miss Laura's weathered cheeks, and her eyes fell shyly away from Martia's.

'I truly hope so,' she admitted, 'because I enjoy visiting him. He likes a rousing argument now and then; says it clears the atmosphere. And I know that's true, because it's like that with me, too.'

'Oh, come now,' Martia derided her lightly. 'I don't believe you ever gave anybody an argument in your life.'

'Ha!' Miss Laura dismissed that airily. 'You should talk to some of the school board back home, and some of the parents of my pupils.'

She grinned and added briskly, 'Well, Mr. Weathersbee is expecting me, so I guess I'd better hurry along. 'Bye now!'

She turned, then remembered something and came back.

'Oh, that poor child, the Conrad girl,' she

68

said. 'How is she?'

'Oh, she's coming along fine.'

'I'm so glad.' Miss Laura's tone was warm and genuine. 'She seemed so unhappy and so mixed up when I visited her. Did she ask that I come back?'

'Well, no,' Martia had to admit. 'But I'm sure she enjoyed your visit a lot.'

Miss Laura cocked her head on one side, like a bird, and chuckled.

'And that, Martia my dear, is probably one of the most inaccurate remarks you ever made, if it's not a downright lie. The girl was rude and bored stiff, and we both know it.'

'But you stayed and talked to her despite that?'

'Well, of course,' Miss Laura agreed without question.

'And of course you forgave her!'

Miss Laura's brows went up in honest surprise.

'Forgave her for the sin of being young and confused? Martia, my dear, that's a sin that only time can erase,' she protested, and went on thoughtfully, 'I've always been a mite impatient with people who claimed that the sins of the present generation should be blamed on their parents. Oh, I admit some parents are to blame when their kids get out of hand. Parents who are too permissive, who are too busy with their social obligations, who won't take time to listen to the children, are to blame for a lot of the things the children do. And I will have to admit I do feel the Conrad child's father should be blamed for what she has made of herself, purely in revolt against him. From what she told me, he really must be a stinker!'

She looked mildly abashed at hearing the word issue from her own lips, and Martia laughed at her.

'Why, Miss Laura! Such language!' she mocked.

Miss Laura grinned an almost girlish grin.

'Well, after all, I have been associated with the young for more years than I care to admit, and some of their chatter inevitably rubs off on a person, no matter how careful she may be,' she defended herself. 'Judging from the Conrad girl's bitterness toward her father, I can't think of a word that describes him more accurately.'

'I can't either,' Martia confessed frankly.

'Essentially, the girl is sound,' Miss Laura said thoughtfully, once more shifting the heavy load in her arms. 'It's just that her energies have been wrongly directed.'

'And being you, you are anxious to help her get on the right track,' Martia accused her.

Deeply in earnest, Miss Laura said, 'If I only could, Martia, I'd feel I'd justified my existence.'

'Why, Miss Laura, what a thing to say!'
Martia protested sincerely. 'As if you haven't
justified your existence for years and years
and years! I'll bet many of your pupils will
agree with me. They must have loved you
dearly for all the fine things you taught
them.'

Miss Laura chuckled wryly.

'Martia, Martia, you've been too long in a
place like this, where your patients are the
elderly. I'm afraid you don't know much
about the younger generation,' she said.
'Love me dearly? They hated the sight of me,
because I made them study when they didn't
want to do anything but play! I was a good
teacher; I admit it without boasting. But I
was not a permissive teacher, accepting
excuses for sloppy homework, for
ill-prepared lessons, for misbehavior in the
schoolroom or on the grounds. What's that
line they use in the Navy? I kept a taut ship.
And they resented it furiously.'

'I suppose they did,' Martia agreed. 'But
when they have children of their own, they'll
wish they could send them to a teacher such
as I know you were. That's when they'll
remember you with affection.'

Miss Laura laughed and patted Martia's
shoulder affectionately.

'Seems you have the ability always to say
the right word at the right time, Martia, my
dear,' she said fondly. 'No wonder the

patients adore you and call you the listening nurse. It always makes me feel better when we have a little chat like this. But I mustn't keep you. And I mustn't keep Mr. Weathersbee waiting.'

Martia walked along the corridor with her toward Jason Weathersbee's room and asked curiously, 'Are you reading aloud to him, Miss Laura?'

'Oh, yes. And, Martia, it's the oddest thing,' Miss Laura confided as they paused outside the closed door. 'I took it for granted he'd want me to read the daily papers to him. But no! He says he's through with that. All he wants to hear nowadays is Westerns, shoot-'em-up Westerns, all about rustlers and cowpokes and bandits and saloon brawls.'

Martia laughed. 'You must enjoy that!'

Miss Laura chuckled, and her eyes were soft.

'Well, the important thing is that he does!' she responded, and added, 'one good thing about Westerns. Justice and right always prevail. I suppose that's the real reason he enjoys them.'

'It's possible,' Martia agreed cautiously, and smiled as Miss Laura tapped gently on the door, and Jason's voice bellowed out, 'Well, come on in. Don't stand out there flapping your jaw!'

The two women grinned at each other as

Miss Laura pushed open the door, and Martia heard Jason growl, 'Well, it's about time you got here. Where the devil have you been?'

The door closed on Miss Laura's answer, and Martia went on about her duties.

It was late in the afternoon when Kirby arrived, and as the door of 329 opened to admit him, Beatsie glared at him with hostile eyes.

'Well, so you finally got here!' she snapped at him.

'Sorry if I'm late.' His tone told her that he wasn't sorry at all, and the hostility in her eyes deepened.

'Late?' she snapped. 'I sent for you hours ago.'

'Did you now?' His eyes and his tone were mocking as he settled himself comfortably in the small blue leather-covered armchair beside her bed. 'Sorry, but I do have a living to make, you know.'

'Doing what?' she demanded.

'Publishing a weekly newspaper, and writing stories about silly girls who smash their cars at the doors of hospitals. Big city newspapers sometimes send me small checks for such stories.'

He was insufferably flippant, his eyes brimming with amusement that only deepened her unreasoning anger that was born chiefly of boredom, since she was in no

73

pain.

'Well, if you'd write up the interview I gave you the first time you were here, you'd make so much money out of it that you could retire and write the Great American Novel,' she sneered. 'Isn't that what all newspaper men yearn to write?'

'Undoubtedly,' he agreed. 'Believe it or not, the thought never occurred to me. And I doubt I'd be allowed to do much writing if I was in jail.'

'In jail? Why should you be in jail?'

'It's very simple. If I'd written the interview the way you wanted me to write it, I'd have been sued for slander and libel. Your father would have received a whopping judgment. I wouldn't, of course, have been able to pay it, so I'd have wound up in jail.'

He obviously thought she was rather simple not to have figured that out for herself.

'Well, every word of it was true,' she snapped.

'From your point of view, I'm sure it was,' he agreed, and added, his tone gentle, 'and I'm very sorry, Beatsie, if it was like that.'

'Well, it was, but you don't have to be sorry for me.'

He was studying her with a curious intentness.

'I don't suppose I do, if it comes to that,' he agreed. 'You're doing a pretty swell job of that all by yourself.'

Her eyes flashed and color burned in her face, against which the patches of adhesive looked very white.

'I am not sorry for myself,' she flashed.

'Maybe not,' he seemed quite unconvinced, 'but I must say you are giving a very good imitation of it.'

She turned her head a little. There was suddenly a mist in her eyes as she burst out, 'Well, what do you expect? I'm lying here all trussed up like a cold Sunday night supper spread out on a table. I can't move my body because of this Iron Maiden they've got me cemented into, my arm is way over my head so I have to eat with one hand, and my face is so stiff that I can't even smile.'

'Do you want to?' His gently mocking voice cut into her angry words, and she stared at him, the mist vanishing beneath the shock of her surprise.

'Want to smile? You blithering idiot! Of course I do!' she blazed at him.

'Then try it,' he suggested infuriatingly. 'It's not nearly as painful as scowling all the time.'

'A lot you know about it!' she flashed.

'Maybe not.' His tone was mildly conciliatory. 'But isn't it worth a try? You might be surprised!'

Sulkily she demanded, 'What's there to smile about?'

'Well, after all, you are going to get well one of these days and be able to be up and around. And when you are, it will be my pleasure to drive you around and show you the sights.'

'What sights?' she demanded sulkily.

'Oh, things like cowboys and Indians.'

'In *Florida*?'

His eyebrows went up in mock surprise.

'Oh, didn't you know? The Seminoles have large herds of cattle and cowboys to ride herd on them.'

'I don't believe it!'

'Fact, I assure you,' he told her. 'Also, you might like to see the wild orchids that grow in trees and are as lovely as anything you'd buy in a fancy flower shop up North!'

She was interested in spite of herself, yet still unwilling to believe him.

'And just where is this fabulous place that not only has cowboys and Indians but wild orchids as well?' she wanted to know loftily. 'Not here at Sunset Acres, I feel sure.'

'Of course not,' he agreed. 'A few miles south in the 'Glades.'

'The 'Glades? What 'Glades?' she puzzled.

'My dear good child!' His surprise now was quite genuine. 'Don't tell me you've never heard of the world-famous Everglades?'

'I've never been on the west coast of Florida before.'

76

'Oh, then you've missed the best part of Florida,' he told her. And even as she would have protested, he went on, 'Oh, you are probably quite familiar with the Gold Coast, Miami and the Beach; night clubs, horse races; dog races; golf tournaments. But over here is the real Florida, as I'll be happy to prove to you as soon as you get out of that Iron Maiden and get the use of your arm again.'

She was staring at him, wide-eyed, no longer hostile and sullen.

'Will you?' she asked in the tone of a child promised a trip to the circus.

'Sure.' He grinned at her. 'It will be my pleasure, if you're a good little girl and eat your spinach and stop yelling at people.'

'I loathe spinach and I don't yell at people!' she snapped truculently.

Kirby sighed.

'Here we go again!' he mused. 'You really are a sassy piece, aren't you?'

'I suppose I am,' she admitted without shame. 'But it's the way I was brought up.'

'It was nothing of the kind!' he cut in firmly. 'It's the way you have developed to get everything you want out of life.'

'Everything I want out of life!' Her voice broke as she repeated his words with an almost hysterical laugh. 'I've never had anything I *really* wanted out of life, from the day I was born! I've told you about that. The thing I wanted more than anything else in the world was that my father love me. He didn't. He hated me.'

'Beatsie, my dear,' Kirby soothed her, genuine pity for her in his voice. 'You've tortured yourself and stuck knives in yourself all your growing-up years because of that! Sure you want love; everybody does. It's the one really important thing in all the world. With it, you have everything, no matter how poor or beat up you are; without it, you have nothing, no matter how rich and important you may think you are.'

She sniffed as though resenting his words, yet once more a mist was in her eyes.

'You sound like one of those silly modern love songs—you're-nobody-till-somebody-loves-you kind of guff.'

Kirby studied her with a curiously intent look before he answered, his tone deceptively mild, 'Ever stop to think, Beatsie, why some songs become so popular that they are sung for years and years and eventually become near-classics?'

'You're going to tell me, I feel sure.' Her voice tried very hard to be sneering, but there was a faint note of curiosity in it.

'Because they state some simple facts that endure for years and years. Take folk songs and such. The rock-an'-roll monstrosities that consist of a long-haired young man yelling, "Yeah, yeah, yeah" and calling it

78

singing will be forgotten next week; and it serves them right. But the ones that tell a truth—those last!'

'Like "You're nobody till somebody loves you"?' Once more she was trying hard to sneer, but it didn't quite come off.

'That's the one. There are a lot of others, too.'

'Sure. I've heard the Lawrence Welk show once or twice when I couldn't escape,' she told him. 'So I suppose I'm nobody, because I'm sure nobody loves me.'

He chuckled, and his chuckle infuriated her. But before she could put her fury into words, he derided her, 'So you're not sorry for yourself! Oh, no, not much you aren't!'

'I am not!' Her voice was shaken, whether with anger or with tears he could not be quite sure.

He leaned toward her and covered her uninjured hand with his own, and his smile was gentle, almost tender.

'Beatsie, my dear, one of these days somebody will love you very dearly, because you will have made yourself very easy to love.'

She wrenched her hand from his, and her eyes blazed.

'Will have made myself?' she repeated as though not quite sure she had heard him correctly.

He seemed surprised. 'Well, of course.

You surely must realize, my dear, that you have quite a job to do on yourself before a man would fall in love with you enough to want to marry you?'

She was all but speechless with rage.

'Why, you—you—' she sputtered furiously.

'The truth always hurts, doesn't it?' His tone was infuriatingly gentle.

'I could have been married half a dozen times if I'd wanted to,' she assured him hotly.

'Oh, but that's against the law,' he teased her.

She was very still for a long moment, and by the movement of her lips he saw she was slowly counting to ten.

'I think,' she told him at last, speaking very distinctly and very deliberately, 'that you are the most infuriating man I have ever known.'

He grinned, adding to her helpless anger.

'Well, anyway, you won't forget me,' he drawled.

'Oh, yes, I will! I'll make it a point to, the very minute I'm out of this place. I'll make it my life's work,' she said through her teeth.

'Good! I'm glad you'll have something to work for. Matter of fact, work might be the very best thing that could happen to you,' he told her. 'I suppose as soon as you are able to travel, you will be leaving Sunset Acres?'

'You can just bet I will! The sooner the

better!'

'I'll buy that!' he agreed. 'Back to New York, I suppose?'

'I don't quite know yet, but I'll think of some place where there are a few people under a hundred years old and where there is a little fun!'

'You'd be surprised what a nice bunch of people you could meet here if you were up and around,' he pointed out.

'You mean there *are* some people here under a hundred?' The sneer now was quite pronounced.

'Oh, quite a few,' he assured her blandly. 'The aides here at the hospital are all young. And there are a lot of young people in the village itself. I'd be happy to introduce you to some of them. You might even like them.'

'I doubt that.'

The twinkle was gone now, and he was studying her gravely.

'Well, of course that would be up to you,' he told her quietly. 'If you wanted to like them, they would like you. If you wanted to look down your nose at them and be the haughty Miss Gotrocks, they would dislike you as much as you disliked them. That's the way things work out in this cockeyed world of ours, you know. Or *do* you?'

He waited for her to speak, and when she did, he was somewhat startled at the complete shift of subject.

81

'I suppose you know my father has abandoned me?'

'I thought it was you who had abandoned him.'

'He sent one of his "legal eagles" out here. He deposited some money in your local bank in my name, and took off like a scalded cat without so much as coming in to speak to me. If that isn't being abandoned, I don't know what is.'

Kirby nodded thoughtfully.

'Well, at least he didn't cut you off without a shilling,' he reminded her.

'He couldn't! The money is from my own estate. My mother left it in trust for me. I wasn't supposed to have control of it for another six months, until I was twenty-one. But I guess he got tired of having me on his conscience and paid me off, the way he did Jutsie!'

Kirby nodded. 'I suppose he is waiting for you to grow up,' he commented.

She stared at him. 'Grow up? I'll be twenty-one in six more months.'

'That's years, not actually growing up. Not the way I see it.'

'Oh? And just what do you see as "growing up"?'

'A few traces of maturity. Those you don't have, my dear.'

She set her teeth hard, and once more she slowly counted to ten, barely above her breath. And once more, when she spoke, he was jolted by her change of tone.

'I suppose marriage is a sign of maturity?' she suggested. 'So you could marry me and help me grow up.'

Kirby laughed, and the laugh brought stinging color to her cheeks.

'Thanks a lot, my dear, but no, thanks!'

She drew a deep hard breath, and her uninjured hand clenched into a tight fist as she fought to steady her voice and made it sound seductive.

'I'm really quite pretty when I'm not flat on my back like this in an Iron Maiden,' she told him.

'Oh, I'm sure you are,' he agreed. 'I've seen pictures of you all done up in your best bib-and-tucker, and you were a delectable dish indeed. And thanks to some pretty fine surgery done here, you're going to be just as pretty again.'

'But you wouldn't like to marry me?'

'I would not. You aren't in love with me, any more than I am with you.'

'But maybe we'd fall in love afterwards!'

Now it was his turn to be angry.

'You really are a brazen little piece, aren't you?'

'I don't mind fighting for what I want. I always have.'

'And did you always get it?'

'Most of the time.'

'Well, your luck has turned, baby!' he assured her as he stood up. 'That is, if you're trying to involve me in a marriage scheme. Because that is definitely all it is. You're trying to drop your father's name so you can have someone else's. And what makes you think I'd be any more willing for you to drag my name in the mud than your father is?'

She made a slightly abashed gesture.

'Well, it was just a thought,' she managed uneasily.

'And probably one of the silliest you have ever had, though I admit that takes in an awful lot of territory,' he snapped at her as he stood up. 'Fall in love *after* marriage! You silly kid, don't you know that you fall in love *first*, and *then* you get married, if you're lucky?'

'In my crowd, marriage is a word to make fun of, and so is love.'

'I have no doubt of that. So I'd say about the smartest thing you can do after you get out of here is find yourself another crowd to run with before something worse than this catches up with you.'

She made a slight gesture with her uninjured hand and asked. 'There could be something worse than this?'

'And don't you ever forget it, my girl! You get married just to change your name and, lady, you don't know what trouble is until it's too late!' He thrust the chair aside and said grimly, 'And that's enough for now.'

There was a gentle tap at the door, and an aide came in with Beatsie's supper tray just as Beatsie asked Kirby anxiously, 'You'll come back?'

Impulsively the aide said, 'Oh, do, Mr. Clarke. She gets so lonely.'

'I do not!' Beatsie flared at her furiously. Kirby grinned at the girl, winked and turned back for a moment toward Beatsie.

'Want me to stay and feed you?' he asked.

'I do not! The stuff they give me here I can eat with one hand, if I can make myself swallow the gook! Which isn't easy, I can tell you!'

The aide, her color rising, placed the tray on the table beside the bed, adjusted it and arranged the dishes, as Kirby made a little farewell gesture with a lifted hand and walked out of the room.

As the door whispered shut behind him, he could hear Beatsie's angry voice denouncing the aide. But there was no answering murmur from the aide, who came scurrying out as fast as she could once she had made the patient comfortable.

'Golly, Mr. Clarke,' the aide murmured, her eyes wide, 'do you suppose all rich people are that hard to get along with?'

'I'm sure they're not, Mary-Sue,' Kirby answered her. 'It's just that Miss Conrad is a very spoiled young woman. But we have to be sorry for her, too.'

'Sorry for her?' Mary-Sue's voice derided that. 'With all her money and her fine clothes and cars and jewels? *Sorry* for her? Whoosh, Mr. Clarke!' And she hurried on to the rack that held supper trays for the other patients.

As Kirby approached the nurses' station, Martia looked up, saw him and came to meet him.

'Well, how's our Miss Conrad tonight?' she asked.

'About as usual, I'd say.' Kirby grinned. 'She's really something, isn't she?'

'Did you quarrel with her?' Martia asked with a touch of anxiety.

Kirby grinned at her. 'Isn't that why you asked me to come to see her?'

Martia laughed softly. 'Well, she was complaining that nobody would, and she seemed to take it as a personal affront.'

'She would! To that one, the whole world is rigged against her, and all she can do is stand and fight back with everything she's got. And right now that's not much but her sharp tongue. But you can't help feeling sorry for her.'

Startled, Martia protested, 'Careful, Kirby!'

Puzzled, he stared at her. 'Careful?'

'You know how dangerous it can be to be sorry for a girl like that,' she reminded him, more than half in earnest. 'She sort of gets

86

under your skin by arousing your pity, and then the first thing you know, she sneaks up on your blind side and moves in for the kill. I don't want that to happen to you, Kirby!'

Kirby laughed as though at some very funny joke.

'Well, relax, Martia, my dear. There isn't the faintest possible chance of that. She has offered to marry me the minute she is free to leave the hospital and promised to have the marriage annulled on the way from the Justice of the Peace! What a gal!'

'What a gal indeed!' Martia marveled. 'One thing is for sure. She believes in the frontal attack. No sitting around waiting for a man to fall in love with her.'

'Any man who did, the way she is now, would be out of his skull!' Kirby said firmly. 'Oh, sure, she's a beauty and all that. But mentally she's about six years old! And I've known a great many six-year-olds who were much more grown up than she is.'

'So have I,' Martia admitted, and smiled at him. 'Well, I guess I don't have to worry about you, then.'

Kirby's brows went up in surprise.

'Do you? Worry about me, I mean?' he asked curiously.

'Well, of course. We're friends, aren't we? At least I hope so.'

'And friends worry about each other's welfare?' There was a faint emphasis on the word 'friends' that Martia was sure she had not heard correctly.

'Well, of course. What else are friends for?' she asked innocently.

He looked down at her, an oddly speculative look in his eyes. And Peter Hayden, emerging from the solarium, paused for a moment, unnoticed, and watched them. He was out of earshot, but their position there in the lobby, silhouetted against the late-afternoon sunset glow behind them, showed him their faces in sharp relief. And his jaw set hard as he jammed his clenched fists into his pockets and strode back to the solarium.

Kirby answered Martia slowly and very thoughtfully.

'Yes, what else are friends for?' he agreed at last, and added briskly, 'I've got to get to work—covering a very fancy party tonight, a box social at the Baptist church to raise funds to send a missionary to the Congo. Considering the conditions as of now in the Congo, it seems like a dirty trick!'

Martia laughed. 'I have to admit you have a point there!'

'I suppose I couldn't persuade you to come along with me? It might be fun, at that.'

Martia shook her head.

'I'm afraid not, thanks. I have to wash my hair,' she told him.

Kirby nodded thoughtfully.

'It's a funny thing, but every time I've ever asked a girl for a date she didn't want to give me, she's always said she had to wash her hair,' he commented dryly.

'Well, it's a thing we do have to do, you know,' she told him lightly. 'You wouldn't want to take us out if our hair was all stringy and uncurled, now would you?'

Kirby said, unexpectedly grave, 'If the girl was you, Martia my sweet, I wouldn't care if her hair was screwed up in a bun and she was wearing sackcloth.'

'Well, aren't you the flattering one!' Martia marveled, her eyes brimming with laughter. 'Be careful, mister. I might take you up on that some day just to prove you don't really mean it.'

'Any time, lady. Any old time at all,' Kirby told her firmly, and walked away.

Martia watched him go and chuckled slightly as she went back to work. He was a dear, she told herself; much too nice to get involved with a spoiled, selfish, undisciplined girl like Beatsie Conrad!

CHAPTER SIX

A few days later, another patient was admitted to the women's ward, and Martia was standing by waiting for her to be brought from Emergency. The woman, the chart indicated, was a Mrs. Blakeston, aged seventy-two and the victim of a bad fall.

When the orderlies came in with the cart, lifted the woman from it, and placed her gently on the bed, Peter Hayden came hurrying in, just as the woman lifted her head and glared with shocked, incredulous eyes at the double row of beds.

'A ward?' she demanded in tones that expressed not only shock but utter outrage. 'This is impossible. I demand a private room!'

Peter said, 'Sorry, Mrs. Blakeston, but there are no private rooms available. And you'll only be here a day or two. Afraid you'll have to make-do with a ward until we can send you home.'

The woman glared up at him furiously, while Martia stood by and looked on, wondering what on earth could be the matter with Peter, who was looking down at the woman with cold, hostile eyes, his clenched fists jammed hard in the pockets of his long white surgeon's coat.

'A day or two?' Mrs. Blakeston demanded furiously. 'In my condition?'

'Your condition is not at all serious, Mrs. Blakeston,' Peter assured her. 'You had a fall when you tripped over a curbstone. You twisted your ankle and bruised your knee and your hands when you flung them out to break your fall. Nothing serious.'

'Don't sound like a fool, young man! I've injured my back!'

Peter shook his head. 'X-rays show no sign of any real damage.'

She glared at him, and Peter's eyes met hers with a cold, unfriendly light that Martia had never before seen turned on a patient.

Mrs. Blakeston's eyes fell first, but she indicated that she was by no means defeated when she snapped, 'I demand that you send for my daughter.'

'Of course,' Peter told her. 'Give the nurse her name and address, and we'll get in touch with her.'

A dark, ugly red crept into the woman's plump, expensively cared for face, and she mumbled, 'My daughter is somewhere in California. She is a Mrs. Michael Adams.'

'California? It's a big state, Mrs. Blakeston. And Adams is not exactly an unusual name,' Peter reminded her. The ugly red deepened.

'You don't have to tell me that,' she snapped. 'My daughter is married to a man named Adams!'

'It's a good old-fashioned name, Mrs. Blakeston. Goes way back to our first ancestor.' Peter was needling the woman, and Martia was more puzzled than ever. 'What city in California? And what business is her husband in?'

'I don't know!' Mrs. Blakeston was goaded into something approaching hysteria. 'I don't know anything about him except he's just a nothing. My daughter brought him home one day and said, bold as brass, "Mother, this is my husband, Mike."'

She turned her head restlessly on the pillow, and slow, angry tears welled from her eyes and slipped down her cheeks.

'Just a nothing!' she repeated, and her voice was shaken with anger. 'Didn't even have a job! Just moved in with us and expected me to support him. I got him a job with my bank, but he only kept it a week. Wanted to be a garage mechanic! Can you imagine? A garage mechanic married to my daughter! Why, Frances had every possible advantage—a fine education, a world tour that we took together so I could show her all the lovely spots where my husband and I spent our honeymoon. She had a fine social position, lovely clothes, everything any sane, sensible girl could want.'

'Except love,' said Peter with a gentleness that was more effective than any angry words could have been.

Mrs. Blakeston stared at him, so shocked and angry that the tears dried. She demanded sharply, 'What do you mean? I adored her! She knew it. And she loved me.'

'That's not the kind of love I meant, Mrs.

Blakeston, as you very well know,' Peter told her. 'You never gave her the chance to meet the kind of man she could love. You just paraded before her a lot of stuffed shirts you would have welcomed as sons-in-law. But do you know something, Mrs. Blakeston? Your love for Frances was so possessive, so selfish, that you wouldn't have accepted any man she wanted to marry. You wanted to keep her tied to your apron strings for the rest of your life so she could be a bitter, lost old maid at your death.'

Mrs. Blakeston listened to him, too stunned to answer, until he had finished. Then she accused him sharply, 'You know my daughter?'

Peter nodded. 'She and her husband came here to see me when they made the arrangements for you to come to Sunset Acres. We had a long talk, and they gave me a very accurate picture of what you have made of their lives during the year they have been married. And it wasn't a pretty picture, either.'

'That's not true! I did everything for them—'

'You did everything you could think of to break up their marriage, and I'm a little surprised that Frances was able to wiggle out from under your thumb long enough to find a man she could be happy with,' Peter cut in.

Mrs. Blakeston said huskily, 'My daughter

came here and talked to you?'

Peter nodded. 'And her husband, too. Quite a decent guy, I thought him, and it was plain to anyone who looked at them that they were deeply in love. Therefore I felt you should not be allowed to break them up.'

Mrs. Blakeston had listened in dawning amazement, and now she demanded eagerly, 'So you know where they are?'

Peter nodded. 'I have their address, of course.'

'Of course? But they didn't think it was worthwhile for them to give it to me, her own mother!' she gasped. 'Then I demand that you wire her immediately and tell her that I need her.'

'You don't, and I'm afraid if you did, I would be inclined to hesitate quite a bit before I wired her or got in touch with her in any way at all,' Peter told her firmly. 'She has made her escape from the cage you built around her, and she has the right to a life of her own.'

She was speechless with rage. After a moment Peter went on, in the tone he was accustomed to use to patients, 'Now, the nurse will give you a sedative to ease your nerves and make you sleep.'

'She'll do nothing of the sort! I don't want to sleep! I demand to have my daughter called,' blazed the old woman furiously.

'Of course, if you prefer, we can send you

94

home immediately,' Peter suggested gently. 'Your housekeeper is waiting to drive you there, if you are ready to go.'

'Hallie is here?'

'Of course.'

Mrs. Blakeston turned her head restlessly and saw that the patients who occupied the other beds were shamelessly listening, fascinated by this break in their dull days.

'Well, what are you staring at?' Mrs. Blakeston snarled at them.

Peter said to Martia, 'The sedative, Nurse.'

'Yes, Doctor,' Martia answered, and picked up the small medication tray on the bedside table. But as she reached for Mrs. Blakeston's arm with the bit of alcohol-moistened cotton, Mrs. Blakeston jerked her arm away and glared at Martia.

'I've told you I don't need a sedative,' she snapped.

Once more Peter's voice was one to which the patients in the hospital were not accustomed.

'Mrs. Blakeston, you are in a hospital, and there are certain rules and regulations that all hospital patients must obey,' he told her sternly. 'I have prescribed a sedative; the nurse is waiting to administer it; and unless you behave yourself, we'll send you straight back home.'

'Home!' Mrs. Blakeston wailed, even as

she submitted reluctantly to Martia's ministrations. 'That horrible little shack!'

'It's the nicest and most luxurious cottage in the entire village, Mrs. Blakeston, and with Hallie to look after you, I'm sure you could be very comfortable, if you'd let yourself be,' Peter pointed out.

He nodded at Martia and walked out of the ward. The eyes of the other seven patients, following him, marveled that the kind, gentle doctor whom they all adored could be so ruthless in his treatment of the newest patient.

Martia waited until the sedative began to take effect; Mrs. Blakeston did not speak, nor did Martia. When she was sure that the sedative was working, Martia slipped from the room, smiling at the other patients before she reached the door and went into the corridor.

Peter was waiting for her, leaning against the wall, hands still jammed deeply in his coat pockets.

'Is the old witch asleep?' he asked.

Startled, Martia said, 'She is getting very drowsy. I'm sure she will be very soon.'

Peter said, 'Let's have some coffee.'

As they walked down the corridor, Peter looked down at Martia and said, 'I suppose you think I was pretty rough on her, don't you?'

'Don't *you*?' Martia answered frankly.

'Not half as rough as she deserved!' Peter's mouth was a thin, angry line. 'I've been expecting her here ever since her daughter and son-in-law came in to see me. Frances said her mother didn't have the nerve to try to destroy herself, but she would manage to cook up some sort of emergency so she could have an excuse for asking that Frances come back to her.'

Seated at the small table in the cafeteria, coffee cooling in its cups before them, Peter lit a cigarette and scowled at the small fire.

'It doesn't seem possible to a sane mind that a mother could love her child so much that she would cripple it emotionally and spiritually just to keep it under her guard, does it?' he mused. And Martia made no answer, because she sensed he was merely speaking his thoughts aloud. 'Frances was twenty-five when she met this Michael. She'd never been allowed to do anything for herself; not even choose her own clothes. She wore what her mother wanted her to wear; she went where her mother wanted to go; she met the people her mother wanted her to meet. In short, at twenty-five she was still a child in everything that really matters. And then one day she was driving on an errand for her mother when the car broke down. I can't think how a car belonging to the Blakeston family would dare, can you? And Mike was the garage mechanic sent out to repair the car. Frances took one look at him and knew he was her man!'

There was silence between them while she waited for him to go on. After a moment he did.

'Fortunately for Frances, it was like that with Mike, too,' he said slowly. 'I can't imagine how they ever managed the courtship. Naturally, they said nothing to me except that somehow they managed to see each other, and when both were sure how they felt about each other, Frances managed to sneak off for an afternoon, and they drove across the state line and were married. And somehow she got the courage to bring him home and present him to her mother.'

He looked up at Martia and grinned suddenly.

'Now there's a scene it might have been interesting to witness, don't you think?' he suggested.

'It must have been really a scene,' Martia agreed, wide-eyed. 'And do you mean that Frances was brave enough at last to defy her mother, after all the years of being under her thumb?'

Peter said quietly, 'I think it was the knowledge of Mike's love for her, and the fact that they were really married, that gave her the courage and the strength to do it. Love can sometimes make people very brave, you know.'

Martia's eyes fell before the look in his, and she said hurriedly, 'So Mrs. Blakeston set about trying to break up the marriage?'

'She began by trying to have it annulled,' Peter answered, turning his coffee cup this way and that, his eyes on the table. 'She offered Mike a pay-off, and Mike practically threw it in her face. Then she pretended to have a heart attack so Frances would not leave her, and insisted they must live with her. And from what Mike and Frances told me, I'm sure there was nothing mean enough or spiteful enough or malicious enough for her not to do, to try to humiliate him in front of her friends and Frances' acquaintances. Frances herself told me that she didn't have any friends; they were all her mother's friends.'

'And even that didn't work?' Martia said quietly. 'Then they really must be deeply in love.'

Peter nodded. 'I'm sure of it, which is why I talked to her as I did,' he answered. And now he was looking straight at her and holding her eyes as his voice deepened and he said in a tone that made her heart leap. 'When two people are deeply in love, Martia, nothing must be allowed to separate them.'

Martia waited, unable to find a word to answer him. And as though he did not really expect an answer, he went on in that slow, deep voice, 'If only one of the two is in love

99

and the other isn't, then that's an entirely different story, of course. But if the one who is in love believes the other one is caged in, hemmed in by old memories and the past, then he just has to fight a little harder to get rid of the ghosts of the past.'

After a moment he looked up at her and asked very gently, 'Do you have the slightest idea what I'm trying to say, Martia?'

'I—I—of course,' she stammered faintly, and added with a note of uneasiness, 'only I just don't quite know what to say!'

He nodded, and his eyes dropped once more to the table.

'Well, of course, Martia, if you are still in love with the past, if the ghost of your first love would always stand between us, which is what I think you may be trying to say, then there is nothing more I can do or say,' he told her, his voice suddenly very weary and very low. 'But if ever in any way you can lay that old ghost, I'll be standing by.'

'No, no, you mustn't,' Martia responded. 'You're much too good and too fine to stand around waiting. There are so many women who would make you the kind of wife you deserve, that you need—'

His slow, unamused grin silenced her and deepened the color in her cheeks.

'Hush that foolishness!' he ordered her. 'Do you suppose I'd have reached the age of thirty-two, unmarried, if just any woman would have satisfied my need for a wife? Don't talk like a child, Martia! I've always been waiting for somebody pretty special. And now that I have found you, I discover that I have to fight a ghost!'

'It's just that loving somebody and losing him hurts so much I can't bear to think of going through it again,' she confessed with a humility that he found deeply touching.

His hand went out across the table and touched hers and closed over it.

'But you wouldn't want a life completely deprived of love, darling,' he told her, an aching tenderness in his low voice. 'The hurt is the price we pay for having loved someone and been loved. And nobody really wants to live without love.'

There was a blur of tears in her downcast eyes that were fastened on their two hands clasped on the edge of the table. After a moment Peter said very gently, 'You wouldn't have missed the happiness you had with Derek, the fun of all the plans you made, all the wonderful hours together. Surely those memories are worth the hurt you suffered when you lost him. At least, darling, you had him for a while. Isn't that something pretty wonderful to remember?'

She raised her eyes to his for a moment, but the ardent tenderness in them made her look down once more.

'Oh, yes!' she whispered, her voice shaken.

'But, darling, memories, even lovely ones, are not food for all of life! You can't go on trying to feed on such husks and starving for reality! Believe me, Martia, it's time you stopped living with your head turned backward, looking over your shoulder, sinking into the past and refusing to accept the present or the future. Martia, the past is past. The present is now. And what the future holds, we have no way of knowing. But we must go forward, not backward.'

'I just don't want to be hurt any more,' she whispered desolately.

He studied her for a long moment, and then he said gently, 'Well, of course you don't, Martia darling. Nobody does. But I've never heard of any way a person could avoid that and go on living.'

'I know,' she confessed humbly. 'But give me a little more time, Peter. Please!'

He nodded, his eyes bleak.

'Of course, darling—all the time you want,' he agreed, and stood up, drawing her chair back as they walked side by side out into the corridor.

A tall, heavily built, ginger-colored woman had been talking to one of the nurses. As she saw Peter, she broke off and came to meet him, anxiety in the brown eyes behind neat rimless eyeglasses.

'Dr. Hayden, I'm Hallie Roberts, Mrs. Blakeston's housekeeper,' she introduced

102

herself. 'How is she?'

'She's fine, Hallie,' Peter answered heartily. 'Matter of fact, you can take her home now if you like.'

Hallie put up a pink-palmed hand in protest and laughed wryly.

'Oh, no, sir, Doctor, not until she wants to come home. That'll be time enough,' she answered, and asked, 'I suppose she wants you to send for Miss Frances?'

Her tone made it a statement rather than a question.

'As a matter of fact, she does,' Peter agreed. 'But of course I'm not going to do it.'

Hallie's face registered a wide smile of sheer delight.

'Well, praise the Lord, Doctor!' She beamed at him. 'I sure hoped you wouldn't. Miss Frances hasn't had a chance for much happiness, and now that she is happy, I sure don't want her dragged back here.'

Peter eyed her sharply.

'You have her address? Miss Frances, I mean? You know where she is?' he asked.

'Don't you, Doctor?' Hallie asked quietly in return.

'Yes,' Peter stated flatly. 'But I have no intention of giving the address to Mrs. Blakeston. Nor must you!'

Hallie's head went up, and there was a trace of resentment in the brown eyes.

'I've no more idea of giving Mrs. Blakeston Miss Frances' address than you have, Doctor,' she told him firmly.

'Well, good for you!' Peter was frankly relieved. 'Mrs. Blakeston's condition is so good that about all she needs is someone to listen to her problems and offer solutions that she wouldn't follow for a million dollars. I see no point whatever in sending for her daughter or for anyone else, as long as you are here to take care of her.'

Hallie said gratefully, 'Thank you, Doctor. I've been taking care of her for more than thirty years, ever since she married. Before her husband died when Miss Frances was just a little child, he asked me to try to keep Miss Frances happy. He felt her mother would dominate her the way she had always dominated him.' She broke off, and her eyes fell in shame. 'I got no business talking like this, Doctor. I just wanted to ask you how she was and when I could take her home.'

'Well, she's fine, Hallie,' Peter answered, and added curiously, 'how did she happen to suffer this fall, anyway?'

Hallie chuckled dryly.

'Oh, she slipped on a scatter rug. The floor was waxed the way she always wanted it, and I guess maybe she wasn't looking where she was going,' she answered frankly.

'Well, she's going to be just fine, and perhaps you can persuade her to let you take her home tomorrow,' Peter told her.

'I'm thanking you, Doctor. I'm thanking you a whole lot for saying you won't bother Miss Frances,' Hallie told him earnestly. 'If she even dreamed her mother was in a hospital, she'd grab a plane and fly right back here, and Mrs. Blakeston wouldn't let her leave again. Miss Frances writes me every week and tells me how happy she is and how well she and Mr. Mike are doing out there. And I don't want to upset them.'

Before Peter could answer, she continued hastily, 'Oh, if she had a bad heart attack, or was really sick or badly hurt or anything, I'd telephone Miss Frances right away. But if there is nothing seriously wrong, then I don't think I will.'

'I wouldn't.' Peter smiled at her. 'And I won't!'

Hallie beamed at him and turned away, hesitated and turned back, anxiety once more in her eyes.

'Excuse me, Doctor, sir, but if at any time you do think Mrs. Blakeston needs Miss Frances, you'll tell me or call her yourself?' she asked.

'Of course I will,' Peter assured her, and the last trace of anxiety vanished from the brown eyes as Hallie moved toward the exit.

Martia watched the woman in her neat dark print dress, her graying head adorned by a small and unobtrusive dark hat, and then she looked up at Peter questioningly.

'So that's an old family retainer of another generation, is it?' she mused aloud.

Peter looked down at her, grinning slightly.

'It would seem so,' he agreed. 'I'd say Mrs. Blakeston was a pretty lucky woman to have a friend as devoted as that, wouldn't you?'

'I would indeed,' Martia answered.

A moment later Peter was called away, and Martia went to the nurses' station to busy herself with the charts. But her thoughts were not on the job, but on what Peter had said to her.

CHAPTER SEVEN

The day came at last, the day Beatsie had told herself glumly never would arrive, the day when she was released from the cast she called her Iron Maiden and her arm was returned to her in perfect condition.

A wheel chair was brought to the bedside, and she was helped into it and wheeled away to the X-ray room. William, who propelled the wheel chairs for all the patients, grinned at her, his dark face flashing a white-toothed smile.

'Sure glad you're getting better, miss,' he

told her as they reached the X-ray room and a white-clad technician came out, smiling warmly at Beatsie.

'Hello, Miss Conrad!' beamed the girl. 'I've been looking forward to this day. Last time I saw you, you were out cold! I'm delighted you are doing so well.'

Beatsie returned the grin and said mockingly, 'What's a nice girl your age doing in this mausoleum?'

The girl's smile faded slightly, but she said sturdily, 'Oh, it takes some of us younger people to look after the older ones. This way, Miss Conrad.'

When Beatsie was stripped and lying flat on her stomach on the treatment table, she moaned, 'This thing has been in the refrigerator. It couldn't be this cold otherwise. And how do you manage to make them so uncomfortable?'

The technician laughed and said, 'Oh, Miss Conrad, we've worked for years to make these tables as uncomfortable as we possibly can.'

'Then you can relax,' Beatsie told her. 'You've succeeded far beyond your wildest dreams.'

When the last X-ray had been made, Beatsie, once more bundled in the ugly, rough hospital gown, was helped back into the chair and wheeled outside to where William was waiting to take her back to her room. Beatsie dropped her hands to the sides of the chair, gave a hard push, and the chair went whizzing down the corridor, with a scandalized William in hot pursuit.

'*Whee!*' shrieked Beatsie as the wheel chair gained momentum on the waxed floor.

All up and down the corridor doors swung open, and nurses and aides emerged into the corridor; but Beatsie, intoxicated by the speed of her ride, bent over the arm rests of the chair and called, 'Out of my way, everybody! Beatsie rides again!'

William caught up with her just as she came to the end of the corridor and, scandalized, but hiding his amusement, said sternly, 'Now that wasn't a bit nice of you, miss. Doctor will ride me ragged for letting you get away from me.'

'Huh!' Beatsie was being wheeled by William back to her own room, where Martia was waiting for her. 'One of these days, William, m'lad, I'm going to get away from the doctor and this place and everybody in it.'

'Yessum, I 'speck you will,' William assured her as Martia held open the door of 329 and looked accusingly at Beatsie.

'Now that was a very childish trick, Beatsie,' Martia tried to scold her. But the girl was too flushed with excitement, too joyous to be downcast.

'I felt childish, Nursie,' Beatsie assured her
108

firmly. 'And it was a whole lot of fun, the most fun I've had since I landed here.'

Martia brought the wheel chair into the room, and William waited to remove it until the girl was back in bed. Instead, Beatsie slid from the wheel chair into the small leather-covered armchair and refused to budge. William grinned at Martia and removed the chair.

Martia said, 'Now, Beatsie, get right back into bed!'

'Huh!' Beatsie thumbed her nose childishly at the bed, gleaming fresh and newly made. 'I've spent all the time in that thing I intend to. I'm up now; the Iron Maiden is gone; and I feel wonderful. I think I'll go out and have my hair done and maybe do some shopping.'

Martia's brows went up.

'Oh, do you now?' she asked. 'I doubt that! Dr. Hayden will have something to say about that, I'm sure.'

Beatsie looked sullen.

'But I must look a sight!' she protested like a disappointed child. 'And I will not go on wearing this horrible rag. Even in a place like Sunset Acres, there must be a few shops where some decent things can be found.'

'How would you like me to have your luggage brought down and let you unpack it?' suggested Martia.

Beatsie cried out, 'Oh, I did have some

luggage, didn't I? I'd forgotten all about it! Oh, yes, if it's still around, have it brought in, and I'll see what I used to think I liked, but will probably hate now.'

'Most likely you will,' Martia agreed.

A little later two handsome airplane-type suitcases had been opened on a small stool before Beatsie, who was absorbed in unpacking.

When Martia came back later in the afternoon, Beatsie had managed to get herself into a filmy rosy-pink nightgown, lined with white, and over it wore a matching negligee of the same lovely colors.

'Well, now, don't you look lovely!' Martia congratulated her, and added, 'Didn't you want some help? You had only to touch the button there, and somebody would have been right along—'

'Whoosh!' Beatsie cut in happily. 'I'm a well woman now, and I don't need help. I'll be leaving soon, won't I?'

'Not very much longer, I think,' Martia answered, and asked impulsively, 'where will you go, Beatsie?'

For a moment the girl's radiant face looked bleak, and Martia was sorry she had asked the question. But after a moment Beatsie said airily, 'Oh, it's a great big wide wonderful world, people keep telling me. I'll think of some place that will be fun.'

But the bleak look was still in her eyes

when Martia left the room.

It was after the supper hour when Kirby Clarke came hurrying down the corridor, tapped lightly on Beatsie's door and pushed it open. He paused in the doorway, looking at the freshly made bed and then at the girl in rosy-pink who sat in the blue armchair, her feet up on the stool that had held her suitcases.

'Oh,' Kirby apologized, and backed toward the door, 'I was looking for Miss Conrad. This used to be her room.'

Beatsie grinned at him happily.

'Come in, you fool! And don't be cute!' she ordered, and indicated a straight chair in a corner. 'Pull up a hassock and set a spell!'

Kirby obeyed her instructions and sat studying her.

'I don't believe it,' he said at last. 'When I was here yesterday, you were still encased in a cast, with your arm above your head.'

Beatsie scowled at him.

'That wasn't yesterday, Kirby, old son! That was a week ago,' she accused him. 'You've been neglecting me shamefully!'

'I'm sorry.' Kirby grinned at her. 'I had to go out of town on business.'

'Blonde or brunette?' Beatsie demanded.

Kirby chuckled. 'With the most beautiful blonde in the country right here, why would I go out of town looking for another one?'

'Then it was a brunette!' she accused him.

'Or maybe a redhead.'

'It was, as I said, my dear girl, a business trip. I had to go over to Miami Beach on a story. And it sort of spread out to Fort Lauderdale and up the coast.'

'Was it a good story?' she asked curiously.

A smile tugged at the corners of his mouth, but he answered her seriously, 'From a newspaperman's point of view, a very good story. I sold it to some of my big-city dailies!'

'Well, hooray for you!' she applauded him mockingly. 'What was it—a jewel robbery? They seem to have a lot of them over there.'

Kirby shook his head. 'A spot of murder,' he told her.

Beatsie's eyes widened.

'Sounds like a "whodunit."'

Kirby grinned. 'Oh, they know "whodunit." Matter of fact, he's under arrest at this moment in the top floor of the Miami jail.'

'Well, well!' Beatsie murmured.

Kirby said, 'I'm delighted to see how well you're getting on. You'll be able to go dancing one of these days.'

'Will *you* take me dancing, Kirby?' she asked.

'It will be a privilege and a pleasure,' he assured her with such conviction that momentarily there was a faint tinge of pink in her cheeks.

'I don't suppose there's any place to dance

in Sunset Acres,' she mourned.

'You'd be surprised!' Kirby told her. 'But we needn't stay here unless you want to. There are some very good night clubs along the coast, and you shall choose the one you like best!'

'You're sweet.' Beatsie beamed at him.

Kirby chuckled. 'Well, I try to be.'

'And succeed beautifully, I'm happy to report,' she answered in a tone as mocking as his had been. Suddenly she became serious. 'Kirby, what do people do here in Sunset Acres for fun?'

'Oh, lots of things,' Kirby answered casually. 'Horseshoe pitching, shuffleboard, fishing—'

'Don't be a goop!' she sniffed disdainfully. 'I don't mean the old people. I know they just sit around and listen to their arteries harden.'

'Did it ever occur to you, my girl, that one of these days you may be an older person and have arteries that act up?'

'Oh, sure,' she dismissed that disdainfully. 'And before you tell me, I'll tell you that I know the only way to keep from growing old is to die young! And that's not an appealing thought, even in my book! But I see young people around. Girls, mostly: the aides; the lab technicians; and some of the nurses. Surely there must be some sort of amusement for them.'

'Well, there's a weekly dance at the Club out on the Point,' he told her. 'And once a month they bring in an orchestra.'

Her pretty mouth curled disdainfully.

'Sounds like a whole lot of fun and games,' she drawled.

'Well, I admit that there are no beatniks there,' he said in reply, his eyes chilling slightly.

She winced at that and lifted her head proudly.

'Maybe you won't believe this,' she told him loftily, 'but I hope I never see another beatnik as long as I live!'

Kirby's brows went up, and there was a gleam of pleasure in his eyes as he answered, 'Well, hooray for you. Maybe being here in Sunset Acres as the victim of a car crash wasn't wasted time for you after all.'

His tone was teasing, and he was smiling at her. But Beatsie was unexpectedly serious when she said softly, 'D'you know something? I don't believe it was.'

Startled, Kirby murmured, 'Well, do tell!'

Color flushed her face, and her eyes took on a defensive light.

'Well, I don't!' she told him. 'I've met some very nice people here. You, for instance.'

Kirby said quickly, 'Hey, now wait a minute.'

Her lip curled disdainfully, though there

114

was an impish twinkle in her eyes.

'Oh, don't cut and run,' she mocked him. 'I'm not going to propose to you again.'

'Well, that's a relief,' Kirby admitted frankly. 'Funny, but I've always felt that was the man's job.'

Beatsie made an airy gesture.

'Of course, theoretically,' she agreed, emphasizing the word. 'But if the man is so stubborn he won't do it, then what's a girl to do? I'm only asking out of curiosity, of course. The whole question is theoretical.'

'A girl could slow down a bit in her mad pursuit.'

'Mad pursuit?' she cut in furiously.

Kirby met her indignant eyes with mild surprise and more than a trace of caution.

'What else would you call it?' he wanted to know.

She hesitated a moment, and her eyes fell.

'I *was* an awful fool at first, wasn't I?' she finally asked so humbly that he was startled.

'Frankly, yes, I'm afraid you were,' he admitted with painful honesty.

Her eyes came back to him at last, and she asked humbly, 'I don't suppose you could be persuaded to believe I've changed?'

He studied her gravely.

'I'd like to, Beatsie. I'd like to very much,' he assured her.

She glowed happily at him.

'Then you just stick around, and you'll

see,' she promised him with an almost childlike eagerness.

'It's a deal,' Kirby promised her just as the door opened and Martia came in.

'Sorry, Kirby, but visiting hours are over,' she told him. And to Beatsie, 'Into bed with you now, young lady!'

'I'm not a bit sleepy!' she protested heatedly. 'I've spent years and years in that bed!'

Kirby said firmly, 'You heard what Martia said. Into bed now!'

'I won't!' Beatsie flared indignantly.

Kirby stooped, lifted her in his arms, tucked her into the bed, and Martia drew the thin sheet up over her.

Beatsie lay perfectly still, staring up at Kirby with wide eyes.

'Quite the cave-man, aren't you?' she tried to sneer, but it didn't quite come out that way.

'When occasion demands.' Kirby grinned at her. 'Always glad to oblige.'

Martia smiled at him, and he said to Beatsie. 'I'll be seeing you.'

'Tomorrow?' Beatsie asked eagerly.

Kirby, on his way to the door, turned and looked at her.

'Tomorrow,' he promised, and went out.

Martia helped Beatsie out of the negligee and tucked her once more into bed.

When Martia came out into the corridor,

Kirby was in conversation with Peter Hayden. As Martia approached, Peter turned to her and said curtly, 'I think you should know about this, too, Martia.'

Kirby turned to Martia with a friendly grin.

'It's just that while I was in Miami Beach on this man-hunt story, I ran into a very interesting character,' Kirby explained. 'That doesn't sound very gracious, but then I don't think she would appreciate it if I tried to be more gracious. Anyway, she is a magazine writer, doing a "spread" on Miami Beach's fiftieth anniversary and bored almost to tears with all the whoop-de-doo! In the course of our conversation at a civic dinner one night, I mentioned Sunset Acres, and she was immediately intrigued. Wants to come over, bring a photographer and do a "spread" on the place, with special emphasis on the hospital, of course. I promised her I'd discuss it with you here, and if it was agreeable I'd telephone her.'

Martia looked swiftly at Peter.

'With Dr. John at that convention in Jacksonville—' she wondered aloud.

Peter scowled, and his tone had a bite in it.

'With Dr. John out of town, I happen to be in charge here,' he reminded her. 'I think it would be a very good idea. Have your friend come over, Kirby, and we'll try to give her some material for the "spread."'

He turned and strode away, and Martia glanced at Kirby, who was scowling after Peter's tall, rapidly moving figure.

'Now what's got his back up all of a sudden?' he wondered aloud.

Martia said, 'I'm afraid I offended him by suggesting that Dr. John be consulted about any write-up of the hospital.'

Kirby looked down at her, and his eyes were narrowed.

'Now that doesn't sound like Peter Hayden. He's not that arrogant or that sensitive, surely,' he protested.

'Then I can't understand what's wrong,' Martia answered, but would not meet his eyes, because in her heart she knew exactly why Peter had been so brusque and unfriendly.

'Oh, well, maybe he's just off his feed or overworked like most doctors,' Kirby decided comfortably. 'I'll gallop along and telephone the elegant Miss Elena Marchant.'

'The writer? I've read some of her stuff; it's very good,' Martia said eagerly. 'Is she very pretty?'

Kirby chuckled. 'In high fashion circles, I gathered from her, the word "pretty" is an insult! According to her, no woman nowadays wants to be called pretty or even beautiful. I believe the proper word is interesting, though I could easily be wrong about that as well as an astronomical number of other things.'

Martia walked with him to the exit, smiled a good night at him and turned back to the nurses' station to go off duty as soon as the day's charts were attended to and her relief arrived.

She was just walking toward the exit when Miss Laura came to meet her, looking eager and flushed and much younger than her age.

'Are you off duty, Martia?' she asked eagerly.

'Yes, Miss Laura, but if there is something I can do—'

Miss Laura would not quite meet her eyes, and her voice was not quite steady when she answered, 'Well, yes, there is, Martia, I want to talk to you, and I thought maybe you would come home to dinner with me. Or we could go to the Inn, if you'd rather.'

Martia's heart sank a little, for she was very tired, as she always was at this time of the evening, after the usual hard and busy day. But she could not refuse Miss Laura, who obviously had something on her mind and was in dire need of somebody to listen.

She smiled and tucked her hand through Miss Laura's arm and said, 'By all means let's make it the Inn. That way, we won't have to cook and to wash dishes afterwards.'

Miss Laura beamed at her. 'That's what I hoped you'd say,' she admitted. 'I'm afraid

I'm not a very good cook. I always get excited when I have company for a meal and seem to forget what little I do know about it. But it's my treat, remember!'

Martia laughed as she followed Miss Laura into the old car and watched her grim expression as she set the car in motion and concentrated so hard on her driving that she did not speak until they had reached the parking lot at the Inn.

'There!' Miss Laura breathed a fervent sigh of relief as she got out of the car, locked the door and stood erect. 'I'm always so relieved when I get to where I'm going without an accident.'

'Why, Miss Laura, you're an excellent driver,' Martia protested quite sincerely as they walked arm in arm up the three shallow steps that led into the wide-winged, quaint old building that housed the Inn and that had stood there for more than fifty years.

Miss Laura looked at her eagerly. 'Am I really, Martia?'

'Well, of course you are, Miss Laura. Why do you doubt it?'

'Well, I guess maybe because I've never gotten over being afraid of a car,' Miss Laura confessed. 'I suppose I have too much imagination. I can look ahead at an intersection and picture what would happen if another car got there at the same time that I did and we didn't see each other!' She shuddered, and Martia laughed and patted her arm gently.

'How long have you been driving, Miss Laura?' she asked.

Wide-eyed, Miss Laura answered, 'Oh, for more than twelve years. And I'm still scared.'

She looked up at Martia and asked anxiously, 'Do you think I should give it up?'

'That's something I can't answer, Miss Laura. You'll have to take the advice of your driving instructor when you go to get your license renewed.'

Miss Laura nodded. 'Yes, I guess that's best,' she agreed.

A pert, pretty waitress in a neat yellow uniform, with a saucy white apron and a matching cap, guided them to a table beside a window that looked out over the Gulf, drenched now in the lovely afterglow of sunset.

When they had ordered and the waitress had gone, Miss Laura looked anxiously at Martia.

'It wasn't about my driving that I wanted to talk to you, Martia,' she admitted, and an unaccustomed flush touched her cheek.

Martia smiled comfortingly at her.

'I'm listening, Miss Laura,' she said.

Miss Laura looked down at the table, and her hands fumbled with the silverware. Obviously she was searching for words that would clothe her thoughts. And Martia, long

121

accustomed to people who wanted her to listen but hardly knew how to start talking, waited.

Finally Miss Laura looked up at her.

'Martia,' she blurted out, 'would you think me a silly old fool if I told you I wanted to get married?'

It was the last thing in the world Martia had expected, and for a moment it rocked her. But the plea in Miss Laura's eyes demanded an answer.

'Of course not, Miss Laura,' she said gently. 'I'd think you were quite normal and very wise; not a silly old fool at all!'

Miss Laura let out a breath of relief so fervent that Martia knew how deeply disturbed she was.

'Well, he's lonely and so am I. And neither of us have a family,' Miss Laura told her. 'And we just thought maybe if we put our two lonelinesses together, we'd find companionship. And that's pretty important at my age, Martia.'

'It's important at any age, Miss Laura,' Martia assured her. 'Who is the lucky man? Do I know him? Somebody in Sunset Acres?'

Miss Laura's color deepened, and for a moment her eyes looked almost frightened.

'It's Mr. Weathersbee,' she blurted.

Martia stared at her, too dazed to be kind.

'Oh, I know,' Miss Laura went hurriedly on as though to give Martia time to recover from the shock. 'You think we are both fools. But he's a very lonely man, and I'm a very lonely woman. And we—well, we get along together, and we respect each other, and I like him. And—well, I don't know why he should, but he likes me, too.'

'Miss Laura, I'm not going to deny that I'm surprised and all that,' Martia told her firmly. 'But I think it's wonderful, and I'm very happy for both of you.'

Miss Laura beamed as the waitress came, serving their dinner. When she had gone Miss Laura looked across the table at Martia and said, 'I suppose people will think we are fools. They'll laugh at us, I suppose, and make jokes about us.'

Martia laid her hand on Miss Laura's, that was still fiddling with the silverware, and said very gently, 'Do *you* mind if people make jokes and laugh at you?'

Miss Laura's head went up, and her eyes flashed.

'Not a bit,' she said firmly. 'And when Jason asked me, and I warned him people would make fun of the marriage of two people our age, he said—' The flush deepened, and a twinkle was in her eyes. 'I won't tell you what he said, because Jason is pretty proficient in profanity, and I wouldn't want to repeat what he said. But it made it pretty plain that nothing anybody can say will bother him.'

'That's about the way I imagined he would feel,' Martia replied.

'Dr. John told Jason before he went to that convention that when he came back, the middle of next week, Jason was going to be discharged from the hospital. And Jason doesn't want to go home alone. He wants me to go with him!' Miss Laura's head went up, and she added firmly, 'And I want to be there.'

'Of course you do, and I think it's wonderful,' Martia assured her with a sincerity that set Miss Laura newly aglow.

Miss Laura dug a fork into her food without interest and then looked back once more at Martia.

'There's one more thing, Martia.' She hesitated.

Martia smiled reassuringly at her. 'Name it, Miss Laura, and if it's possible, consider it done!'

'We'd like to be married in the hospital,' said Miss Laura, and all but held her breath as she awaited Martia's answer.

'Why, that's fine, Miss Laura,' Martia told her quickly. 'I'm sure there couldn't possibly be any objection from anybody on the staff.'

'Jason wanted to talk to Dr. John before he left, but I made him wait because I wanted to be sure I knew what I was doing.' Miss Laura grinned impishly. 'Truth is, I wanted to talk to you, Martia, and see what you thought. Now that I know you don't think we are a couple of old fools, there's nothing in the way of our marriage.'

Martia said uneasily after a moment of deep thought, 'Miss Laura, you know I wouldn't hurt your feelings or upset you for the world, don't you?'

The question obviously surprised Miss Laura, who eyed her curiously.

'Why, of course not, Martia,' she protested. 'You're the kindest, sweetest person alive. And if you think I shouldn't marry Jason—'

'I only wanted to point out, Miss Laura, that Mr. Weathersbee is not the easiest man in the world to get along with, and that you should know what you were letting yourself in for,' Martia said awkwardly.

Miss Laura's laugh was carefree as she caroled gaily. 'Oh, I can manage him. He doesn't know it yet, but *I* do. So don't worry about that, Martia.'

Martia studied her for a moment, amused at the thought of what Jason Weathersbee's reaction would have been to that remark. Then she laughed and said, 'D'you know, Miss Laura, I really think you can! So my best wishes to you and my congratulations to him. He's a very lucky man.'

Miss Laura sat erect and gave her attention to her food, as though, now that she had relieved her mind of the problem that had been bothering her, her appetite had returned.

'I can't think what the staff and also the patients at the hospital will say,' she commented at last as though it were a matter of no importance whatever to her.

'I've just thought of something, Miss Laura,' Martia said when their dessert had been served. 'There's a very well known writer for a big news-weekly magazine coming over in a few days to do an article about Sunset Acres. How would you and Mr. Weathersbee like to be "written up" in the article?'

Miss Laura looked startled.

'Oh, I don't know, Martia,' she said. 'I'd have to ask Jason.'

'I'm sure Miss Marchant would be very interested in a wedding in the hospital,' Martia told her, smiling. 'But if you'd rather we didn't mention it to her, that's quite all right. The decision has to be yours and Mr. Weathersbee's, of course.'

Miss Laura was obviously still turning the thought over in her mind, and at last she said thoughtfully, 'Well, come to think of it, if I'm going to manage Jason, I can't begin too early. And besides, a write-up in a news magazine will be the best and easiest way to let all our friends know. I meant only to tell that nice young Kirby Clarke, but this will be much better! We'll have the wedding while she's here, and she can take pictures, and Jason and I will have them and the article for the rest of our lives together.'

She beamed at Martia, who told herself privately that Mr. Weathersbee's days of being a rough-tongued, irascible, difficult old man were numbered. Miss Laura would ride over him like a gentle bulldozer—and best of all, she would make him love it! Of that Martia was quite sure.

CHAPTER EIGHT

It was several days later, as Martia and Peter were completing their morning rounds, that Kirby entered the main corridor, accompanied by a tall, fashionably thin, elegantly attired woman. A plump, ruddy-faced young man with a camera followed them.

'Hello, Peter, Martia,' Kirby greeted them with a beaming smile. 'Miss Marchant, meet the mainspring of the hospital. Dr.Peter Hayden; Nurse Martia Stapleton.'

The woman smiled briefly at Martia and turned to Peter, her hand extended to meet his and her smile warming as her eyes swept over him from the top of his dark head to the tips of his shoes.

'Hello, Peter; I'm Elena,' she brushed

aside any formalities without an instant's hesitation.

Peter grinned and gave her hand a firm pressure.

'Hello, Elena,' he answered in kind. Kirby grinned at Martia, and his brows went up in a quizzical insistence that she share his mirth.

'And this is Bill Kimble—' Elena waved a hand carelessly at the young man with his cameras—'the best cameraman in seven states.'

The young man eyed her sourly and said, 'Put that in writing on the boss' desk sometimes. It might even get me a raise.' And before she could answer, he greeted the others, 'Hi, folks.'

'I've been fascinated by what Kirby has been telling me about this place, Peter,' Elena told him, as though no one else were there. 'Not alone the village, but most of all the hospital. It's sweet of you to let us cover this in our "spread." I'm very grateful.'

'We're pleased to have you here, Elena, and Bill, of course,' said Peter.

'Well, now that all the formalities are over and everybody knows everybody else, I'll be running along,' said Kirby. 'Got to put the paper to bed.'

'But aren't you going to say hello to Beatsie?' Martia protested. 'She'd never forgive you if you didn't.'

Although Elena had been apparently absorbed in Peter, she caught the name and turned swiftly, bright-eyed.

'Is that the Conrad girl? Oh, I simply must talk to her,' she announced as though there couldn't possibly be any objection from anybody, least of all Beatsie herself.

Peter glanced at Martia questioningly, and Martia said quietly, 'I'll see how Beatsie feels about being interviewed.'

'Oh, I don't want to interview her.' Elena laughed. 'She's not nearly that important. I'd just like to see what she looks like after that car crash.'

Martia stared at her and then at Peter. Then, with her head high, she walked to Beatsie's door and opened it.

Beatsie was in her chair, a crossword puzzle on her lap, her golden head bent above it.

She looked up as Martia came into the room and said, frowning, 'Hey, what's up? You've just been in here. I thought I'd been poked and examined and pushed around enough until evening rounds.'

Martia smiled at her. 'There's a woman here doing an article about the village, with special emphasis on the hospital, and she wants to meet you.'

'Who is she?'

'A woman named Elena Marchant.'

Beatsie's brows drew together as she tried

to remember. Suddenly she said, 'Oh, yes. She writes for the *Weekly Monitor* and has interviewed my old man. She's here?'

'Outside in the corridor.'

Beatsie was still for a moment, and then she lifted her chin and said, 'Well, trot her in.'

Martia hesitated. 'You'll behave yourself, Beatsie?'

Beatsie gave her an impish grin.

'You mean you don't want me to slug her?'

'I certainly don't, and I'm sure Kirby wouldn't either. He's the one that brought her here.'

A very thoughtful look touched Beatsie's eyes, and she was silent for a moment. Then she grinned and said, 'So be it. I've been wanting to practice my newly acquired ladylike virtues on somebody, and I can't think of anybody I'd rather use 'em on than the elegant Elena! Trot her in.'

'Promise?'

Wide-eyed, Beatsie said, 'Promise!' and made an absurd, childish gesture of crossing her heart.

Martia opened the door into the corridor and said pleasantly, 'Miss Conrad will see you now, Miss Marchant.'

Elena stiffened and her eyes flashed.

'Oh, will she? That's very kind of her, Nurse!'

She swept past Martia, the crisp sharkskin of her smartly cut and extremely brief frock trying hard to be a sweeping train. Bill, leaning against the corridor wall, chuckled warmly, winking at Martia and holding up his hand, thumb and first finger in a gay salute.

Martia glanced at Peter, who was watching her with a curiously speculative look as though not quite sure what to make of her. Then he said crisply, 'I'll be in my office when Miss Marchant is ready to make the tour of the hospital.'

'Yes, Doctor,' said Martia without expression.

Kirby had vanished, and Martia hesitated, not quite sure whether she should follow Elena into Beatsie's room or go on about her duties. Since the voices of the two behind the closed door were merely a murmur, it seemed safe to leave them alone.

As Martia moved toward the nurses' station, Bill trailed her and leaned against the counter, eyeing with frank appreciation the aides and nurses who were elaborately unconscious of his regard.

'Funny, I fought like the devil when Boss-Lady told me we were coming over here to do a spread on a retirement village and a hospital for geriatrics,' he mused almost as though to himself. 'I thought everybody would be at least a hundred and two years old, and I'd waste my plates. But you've got some livin' dolls running around here!'

He was so matter of fact, so completely without the faintest intention of being offensive, that Martia found herself liking him.

'It takes the younger generation to wait on the older one,' she reminded him.

He glanced at her as though he had almost forgotten she was within earshot.

'Oh, sure, sure, I guess so,' he agreed. 'But I'd think the oldsters would prefer to have other oldsters look after them.'

Martia said lightly, 'Oh, our oldsters aren't all that old! As a matter of fact, we are having a wedding here Sunday afternoon.'

Bill asked, 'You and the doc?'

Martia gasped, and color poured into her face.

'Certainly not,' she flashed, and went on hurriedly, 'two of our residents. One is a patient; the other is a retired schoolteacher who has always been so proud of her perfect health that she puts in a lot of time here in the hospital, doing small services for the patients.'

'And she snagged herself a husband!' Bill mused, his eyes brightening. 'Nice going for the old girl!'

Martia stiffened, and her eyes cooled.

'Please understand that if this is included in the article, there is to be no ridicule, nothing that would embarrass them,' she warned him.

Bill put up a protesting hand.

'Lady, I don't have anything to do with writing the article,' he assured her. 'All I do is take the pix. When we get back to Manhattan, the boss throws out the ones I liked best and makes his own selection. You'll have to make your plea to the elegant Elena, not to me.'

'That I shall certainly do,' Martia told him firmly.

So when Elena emerged from Beatsie's room, a smile of a cat that had breakfasted on the family's coffee cream on her generously lipsticked mouth, Martia went to meet her.

'That's quite a gal in there,' Elena murmured, her eyes still amused. 'You really must have done a fine job on her. She looks much better than when I saw her last. She behaves better, too.'

'You've known her before?' asked Martia.

'Of course. I interviewed her father and I covered—you should excuse the expression, but I can't think of a better one at the moment—her debut, which was quite a brawl. I think every half-starved beatnik for miles around was there. Her father was quite upset. And that happens to be the understatement of this or any other century.'

Bill said briskly, 'Too bad, Boss-Lady,

133

that we don't plan to be here Sunday.'

Elena studied him curiously.

'Who says we don't?' she asked icily.

'I thought we were due back in New York on Sunday.' Bill sounded aggrieved.

Elena studied him and then looked at Martia, airy brows raised.

'What's going to happen Sunday that Bill and I should know about?' she demanded. Her tone was curt, as though she were speaking to an inefficient servant.

'A wedding.' Martia's tone was equally curt.

'A wedding?' Elena repeated. And then, her eyes widening, 'You don't mean Kirby and the Conrad girl?'

Martia shook her head. 'A patient and a resident of the village. Senior citizens. They met here at the hospital, and now they are going to be married and want it to take place here where they first met.'

Elena thought about it for a moment and then nodded.

'Might give a nice romantic touch to the spread,' she mused. And to Bill, 'We stay for the wedding.'

Bill shrugged and heaved a deep sigh.

'There's one thing you must promise, Miss Marchant,' said Martia.

Elena's eyes chilled, and her head went up as she surveyed Martia from head to foot.

'*I* must promise *you* something, Nurse?'

134

Her tone was biting.

'Just that you won't ridicule the bridal couple, that's all.'

'My dear girl!' Elena's tone was haughty. 'Nobody, not even my editor, tells me how I shall handle a story. And I certainly have no intention of allowing an outsider to do it.'

'I'm not quite an outsider as far as the hospital is concerned, Miss Marchant,' Martia insisted stubbornly. 'And unless you agree not to make fun of them, I'm afraid you won't be allowed to attend the wedding.'

'Allowed to? Why, you ridiculous creature! You aren't in charge of the hospital! I feel sure that nice young doctor will have something to say about all this. Where is he?' Outrage and astonishment vied for primary in Elena's voice.

'He's in his office, Miss Marchant. I'll show you the way,' Martia began, but Elena brushed her aside.

'Don't bother! I'm sure I can find it and him, and perhaps see quite a bit of the hospital you'd rather I wouldn't see!' she snapped, and ordered, 'come along, Bill!'

Bill shouldered his camera, grinned ruefully at Martia and murmured just above his breath, 'My Boss-Lady's voice! The laws of the Medes and Persians were written in water, compared to her orders! See you around, ma'am.'

Martia drew a deep, hard breath and stood

very still, wishing with all her heart that she had not mentioned the wedding planned for Sunday, yet knowing that if she hadn't, Elena would have heard it from someone else.

It was late afternoon before she had a chance to talk to Peter. Elena and Bill had left shortly after noon, and Peter had been very busy. Or, wondered Martia forlornly, was he just keeping out of her way? Instantly she corrected that thought and told herself she was being a silly idiot. It had been a very busy day, and the interruption of Elena's visit had added to the rush.

She looked up with relief when Peter came striding down to the nurses' station, consulted a couple of charts and, as he handed them back to her said, very casually, 'Oh, I hope you are free for dinner tonight?'

Martia glowed happily. 'Oh, yes, I am.'

'Good!' said Peter, and went on briskly, 'Miss Marchant and the cameraman are staying at the Inn over the week-end, to attend the wedding on Sunday. I asked them to have dinner with me, and I thought if you were free, you might like to come, too.'

Martia felt as though she had been slapped, even while she realized how silly she was to harbor such a feeling. He was watching her, and she managed to keep her expression steady as she said quietly, 'Thank you; I'd like to. And there is something I

136

wish you would discuss with Miss Marchant.'

Peter's brows went up in question, and Martia continued doggedly:

'It's about the wedding Sunday. I just wanted her to promise that she wouldn't—well, ridicule the couple, make fun of them.'

'Now why on earth should she do that?' he cut in sharply.

Martia answered stiffly, 'Miss Laura is afraid people will laugh at two people their age getting married.'

'Oh, I don't think you need worry about Elena's story.' Peter spoke as though he had known the Marchant woman for years, Martia told herself. 'She's a very warm-hearted, sympathetic person, and I'm sure she will handle the story beautifully. She's really quite an accomplished writer, you know.'

'Yes, I know.' Martia's tone was colorless.

He was studying her with a curiously reflective glance. But Martia's eyes were downcast and her expression completely unreadable.

'I introduced her to Mr. Weathersbee and Miss Laura,' he went on. 'She agreed with me that their reasons for taking this step were easily understandable and, in fact, quite touching. Loneliness at their age can be a very bitter thing.'

'I only wanted to be sure she doesn't hurt their feelings,' Martia managed, a faintly defensive note in her voice.

'I'm sure you needn't worry about that,' Peter answered. 'She agrees with me that people who try to live in their memories and refuse to face up to the present run a very good chance of feeling the loneliness Miss Laura and Mr. Weathersbee are experiencing. Only their luck turned when they least expected it, and now they are getting another chance at companionship and happiness.'

She looked up at him for a moment and saw the hint of a shadow in his eyes. And her heart leaped at the thought that he was still in love with her. Or was he? She was almost afraid to follow up that thought. After a moment he turned and walked back down the corridor.

Martia dropped down on the stool beside the large file of charts and for a moment felt a tremor shake her tired body. Had he meant that last warning about loneliness for her, or for himself? Was he indicating that perhaps he was growing tired of waiting?

CHAPTER NINE

Elena piloted the sleek, gleaming car neatly into the parking space and sat for a moment looking about her with every evidence of delight. It was that hour of the day that had long been Martia's favorite, after sunset but not yet dark.

Tall palm trees stirred faintly in the breeze from the Gulf, and ancient live oaks, their gigantic branches dripping with Spanish moss, stirred faintly as if in sympathy with the palm trees.

The Lodge, long, low, wide, was aglow with soft lights. As Peter helped Elena from the convertible, she looked about her, drawing a deep breath of sheer delight.

'But this is lovely,' she enthused. 'Bill, we must have some pix.'

'Sure, Boss-Lady, sure,' Bill said with weary docility as he helped Martia out of the car. 'First thing in the morning.'

'This is much too nice for your geriatrics, Peter dear.' Elena tucked her hand through his arm as they moved toward the steps that led into the Lodge, and added hastily, 'Oh, I don't mean that they don't deserve the very best or appreciate it, because I'm sure they do. But we must have driven several miles out of the village. Isn't it a bit difficult for them to get out here, unless, of course, they have cars and can drive?'

'Oh, the Lodge isn't a part of the village,' Peter answered. 'It's open to them, of course, any time they want to come out. But it's really a place that caters to people from all over the area; not just the villagers.'

'Oh, I see,' said Elena. And over her shoulder, without turning her head, she said to Bill, 'Skip the pix, Bill.'

'Sure, Boss-Lady, sure,' Bill responded and winked at Martia as they followed Peter and Elena up the three wide, shallow steps and into the Lodge.

Although it was early, the dining room was already well-filled, and a few couples were dancing in the cleared space beyond the tables to the music of a juke-box.

A plump, middle-aged man, ruddy-faced with sun and good living, his white dinner jacket immaculate, greeted Peter and Martia by name and was introduced to Elena and Bill. He guided them to a table beside a window and snapped his fingers at a passing waiter, who sprang to instant attention.

'You order, Peter,' Elena cooed sweetly at him. 'It's obvious you are not a stranger here, so you'd be more likely than Bill and I to know what's good.'

The waiter proffered a large menu, and Peter gave the order briskly, pausing politely to consult the others. When the waiter had

140

gone, Elena studied him curiously as he bent forward, lighter in his hand, to ignite her cigarette.

'You come here often, Peter?' she asked.

Peter laughed ruefully.

'Not as often as I'd like,' he told her, 'but as often as I can.'

Elena's eyes flicked to Martia. For a moment the eyes of the two women held, and there was the bright flash of animosity between them; a look that was like a two-edged sword. Elena's eyes fell first, and Martia turned to Bill with some bright bit of small talk.

The music ended, and the couples sought their tables. A little later, the music began again, this time a Strauss waltz, and Elena looked eagerly at Peter.

'Oh, Peter, a waltz! Could we dance?' she asked with pretty eagerness.

'Of course,' said Peter as he stood up and drew back her chair. 'That's if you don't mind my stepping on your feet a bit. I'm a bit rusty, I'm afraid!'

Elena laughed up at him as she tucked her hand through his arm.

'I don't for a moment believe it, Peter dear, but step on my feet all you like!' she trilled gaily as they passed out of earshot and the music claimed him.

Bill looked at Martia and grinned wryly.

'I'd ask you to dance, honey-bun,' he told

her frankly, 'but my feet hurt.'

Martia laughed and answered, 'So do mine. I'd rather just watch.'

Elena and Peter were dancing very close. Her face was tilted upward, laughing, and Peter was looking down at her with every evidence of being very well content with the world as he saw it at the moment.

Bill, watching Martia, said quietly, 'I only hope Doc is as smart as he looks.'

Startled, Martia turned to him, her brows raised.

'Now what is that supposed to mean?' she demanded swiftly.

Bill met her eyes, his round, plump face all but expressionless.

'Only that Elena is on the prowl, and that could mean disaster for a man not smart enough to realize it.'

Martia felt her face grow warm with color, and her eyes turned from his to the dancers. But Bill was watching her steadily, and after a moment she went on in that quiet, gentle voice.

'Of course if he's smart enough to see what a phony she really is, then you have nothing to worry about, honey-bun.'

Martia caught her breath and stared at him.

'Why should I worry?' she began hotly, but Bill's grin stopped her protest before she could finish.

142

'Oh, I sort of got the impression Doc was your own exclusive property,' he said mildly.

'Well, you got the wrong impression,' Martia told him curtly.

'Sure, sure, sure.' Bill's tone was gently polite but unconvinced. 'I just wanted to tell you that as soon as she's finished with him, she'll toss him back, and he can be all yours again. That is, if you want him.'

Martia studied him with a sudden sharp clarity.

'You dislike her, don't you?' she asked.

Bill's sandy brows went up, and he scrubbed out his cigarette in the tray before him, his eyes on the small task until he was sure every last spark had been killed off.

'Well, no, I don't dislike her,' he countered. 'I hate her insides!'

Martia asked, 'Then why do you work with her?'

Bill grinned sourly.

'I knew you'd ask that,' he admitted. 'I work with her because she gets all the best assignments, and the office doesn't dare question any of her expense accounts, and that means they can't question mine, either. I'm building up a reputation, thanks to working with her, so I grit my teeth and take her orders until I can go out on my own. And that's a day I'm looking forward to, believe me, because that will be the day when I can lay it on the line and tell her what

I really think of her!'

Impressed, Martia said quietly, 'It must be very unpleasant working with her when you dislike her so much.'

Bill grinned that sour smile and lit another cigarette.

'Oh, I can take it for a while longer,' he told her, 'but I just wanted to warn you that you're going to have to ride herd on your Doc while she's here. And incidentally, where is she? And where is he? I don't see them on the floor.'

Martia searched the crowd, but there was no sign of Peter and Elena. And when finally they came back, Elena wore the look of a cat well satisfied with the family's morning cream, and Peter had an odd look that Martia could not quite analyze.

'Peter's been showing me the most fascinating flower,' Elena chirped gaily. 'What was it again, Peter?'

'A night-blooming cereus,' Peter answered as he sat down between her and Martia. 'It was scheduled by the parking lot attendant to be in full bloom at nine, so we waited to watch it.'

'And it's simply amazing!' Elena chattered happily. 'The size of an electric light globe, at first it's a tight bud. Then, gradually, it stirs and begins to enlarge, and the petals curl down.'

'They are lovely, aren't they?' Martia said

coolly.

Elena looked at her as though realizing for the first time that she was there.

'Oh, you've seen them?' she asked.

'Of course. Many, many times. I've lived here for years,' Martia answered. She turned deliberately to Peter and said softly, but quite coolly, 'Forgive me, Dr. Hayden, but that lipstick does nothing for you. It's much more becoming to Elena.'

Peter made a startled gesture, wiped his cheek, and Elena laughed.

For a long moment Peter and Martia looked straight at each other, and then Martia turned to Bill with a light remark. For the rest of the evening, Martia was aware of Peter's eyes on her with a curiously speculative look. It was almost, she told herself uneasily as though he saw her for the first time. Perhaps he was comparing her to the devastatingly elegant Elena. Martia told herself that Elena was not lovely; but she was very distinguished-looking, almost startlingly so. And to any man who looked at her, she must seem like a dazzling creature indeed.

Martia set her teeth and managed not to meet his eyes lest her own fill with tears. For to weep here in the presence of a woman she knew was her enemy would be unbearably humiliating.

When dinner was over, Peter and Elena had danced again, then came back to the table. Without sitting down, Peter said with a pleasant smile, 'Well, much as I hate to end such an exciting evening, I'm afraid I must get back to the hospital.'

Elena looked stricken. 'Oh, but, Peter darling, it's early yet! Why, it can't be more than nine o'clock!'

Bill consulted his wrist-watch and said firmly, 'It's a quarter to ten.'

Elena shot him an ugly glance and purred at Peter, 'You see, darling, it's really quite early, much too early to break up the party.'

Peter smiled at her.

'I have a couple of patients I want to look in on before bed check,' he told her. 'But there's no reason the party should break up. I can call a cab.'

'Nonsense!' Elena said, and her voice had a faint edge as she looked down at Bill and Martia. 'When you leave, darling, the party is over.'

She gathered up her bag and gloves and turned toward the door.

Bill grinned at Martia as he drew her chair back. When she rose, he tucked her hand firmly through his arm, and they followed Peter and Elena out to the parking lot and into her car. Bill and Martia got in the back, Peter and Elena in front. Then Elena shot the car out of the lot and down the wide, sandy road with its border of ancient live oaks, their curtains of moss swaying like

146

ghosts through the soft night air.

At the hospital, Elena drew up to the entrance. As Peter got out, Elena looked over her shoulder at Martia.

'Aren't you getting out here?' she demanded coolly.

'Of course,' said Martia, and let Bill help her out and walk her to the steps.

Peter lingered beside the car to say good night to Elena, and Bill grinned down at Martia and said softly, 'Thanks a lot for a lovely evening, honey-bun. I only wish I lived close at hand so I could pursue you relentlessly, like it says in the story-books. But then you probably wouldn't give me a tumble, even if I camped on your door step the rest of my life.'

And Martia said with a frankness that made Bill chuckle, 'I'm afraid not, Bill. But thanks for everything.'

Elena called from the car, 'Unless you want to walk back to the Inn, Bill, come on!'

'Sure, Boss-Lady,' answered Bill, and bent his head, brushing Martia's cheek with his lips before he turned and strode toward the car.

Martia waited on the wide, shallow steps until the car had driven off and Peter came to join her.

'There goes a woman who gets what she wants out of life, wouldn't you say?' She could not keep back the words. Peter looked down at her, his face in shadow against the soft light that spilled out from the lobby.

'Well, no, I wouldn't say that. At least she doesn't always, I'm sure. But then, does anybody?' Peter drawled.

She looked up at him, startled by his tone. But before she could manage an answer, he went on briskly, 'You'd better run along to bed and get some sleep. Want me to walk you to the dorm?'

'Oh, of course not, Doctor,' Martia assured him politely. 'I waited because I didn't know whether you would need me, with the two patients you have to see.'

'Why no, I don't think so,' he answered briskly. 'There are a couple of night nurses on duty if I need help. You run along, and I'll see you in the morning. Good night.'

He strode past her into the hospital, and Martia turned along the narrow, well-lit path that led the short distance to the dormitory. There, in her own small room, she dropped down on the side of the bed and put her face in her hands.

The evening had been a most disturbing one. She realized that Elena was the first attractive woman in his own age bracket that Peter had met since he had come to Sunset Acres. He had been attracted to Martia because she was young, attractive; and she had had no competition. Only two of the other nurses were unmarried, and they were

148

middle-aged. So it had been Martia with whom he had thought himself in love.

Thought himself in love?

She writhed beneath the cruel impact of that thought, and yet she made herself face it. For it could easily be true. She recalled the way he had looked at her when she had commented dryly on the lipstick on his cheek, almost as though he had never seen her before. Well, maybe he had looked at her with the feeling that he *was* seeing her for the first time; seeing her beside Elena, who was everything that Martia was not!

It had been, she recalled, the spur of jealousy that had moved Peter to tell her that he loved her. He had been jealous of Kirby. Now Martia knew that any doubt of her love for Peter had fled before the spur of her jealousy of Elena. She had liked Peter from the first day they had met; she had respected his ability as a doctor and a surgeon; but she had fled in panic from the thought of falling in love with him, even when she knew there was some danger of him falling in love with her!

Danger! The word made her laugh a small, bitter laugh. Because now that she had seen him with Elena, now that she had known the sharp bite of jealousy, she knew that she loved Peter. No matter what the future might hold, she would be in love with Peter Hayden, as once she had been in love with Derek. But then she had been much younger. It had been first love; that love between two young people that is all gossamer wings and silver moonlight and that rarely can endure the sunlight of marriage. With Peter, life could be glorious; a song of delight. Without Peter, nothing would matter very much.

CHAPTER TEN

The entire hospital had been rocked with an unaccustomed and very pleasurable excitement by the news of the engagement of Miss Laura to Jason Weathersbee.

Martia came into Jason's room Sunday morning and smiled warmly at him.

'Well, this is the big day, Mr. Weathersbee,' she told him lightly as she checked his chart.

'All this whoop-de-doo and nonsense!' he growled from his wheel chair. 'You'd think two people our age could get married without all this, wouldn't you? I suppose everybody is snickering and making jokes.'

'That's not true at all, Mr. Weathersbee,' Martia protested warmly. 'We are all happy for you and Miss Laura, and, of course, it's a very welcome break for all of us in our rather routine days. But I can assure you nobody is snickering or making jokes. We think it's wonderful that you have found each other at last.'

Jason looked out of the window and said quietly, 'I'm really a very lucky man, wouldn't you say?'

'Of course you are, Mr. Weathersbee,' Martia assured him with a sincerity he found very pleasing. 'And Miss Laura is a very lucky woman, too!'

Jason considered that for a moment, and then he nodded.

'Well, she is at that, isn't she?' he admitted frankly.

Martia laughed and went her busy way.

The solarium was a pleasant, sunny place facing the Gulf. Bright-colored chintz cushions filled the wicker chairs and settees, and rattan tables held piles of magazines and ash trays and large pots of growing plants. But today the chairs and settees and tables had been pushed back, the room was filled with flowers banked against the walls, and against the wide windows an improvised altar had been set up.

Dr. John had returned the night before and had been briefed on what was about to take place. He had been delighted, had congratulated Jason warmly and had offered to give the bride away.

Jason had snorted, but Dr. John had said firmly, 'It's what any bride has a right to expect. And as your oldest friend and hers, I insist on the privilege!'

Jason glared at him, and then his expression softened.

'You're a good guy, John,' he admitted.

Dr. John laughed.

'Coming from you, that's quite a compliment!'

Jason made a gesture with a hand that had never been any stranger to hard work and growled, 'Oh, well, I always believed in giving credit where credit was due! You've got to admit that.'

'I do, Jason, I certainly do.' Dr. John agreed. 'Well, I'll see you in the solarium at four P.M.'

'I'll try to be there.'

'Oh, don't worry about that. We'll see to it that you are there, old man. The exits are all under guard and you can't get out of this place no matter how smart you are! Four P.M., and don't suffer any change of heart at the last minute, will you?'

'Under the circumstances, I wouldn't dare.' Jason grinned, then became entirely serious, 'I'm really a very lucky man, John, and believe me, I know it!'

'That's good, Jason.' Dr. John's tone matched his. 'I agree with you. You and Miss Laura are both lucky.'

Under orders, Miss Laura arrived a little after two.

Martia was waiting for her and smiled at her.

'I don't understand, Martia. Why did I have to be here so early?' Miss Laura wondered.

Martia put an arm about her and guided her toward room 329.

'You'll find out, Miss Laura,' she responded to the older woman's bewilderment. 'Beatsie has a surprise for you.'

She opened the door, guided Miss Laura into the room and said gaily, 'Here she is, Beatsie!'

'Well, at last!' Beatsie fumed. 'I was beginning to think you'd changed your mind and had run out on us and the Weathersbee gent.'

'Why, Beatsie, how could you possibly think—' Miss Laura's voice broke off in a startled gasp as she looked at the boxes on the bed, from which were spilling a variety of feminine garments.

'For you, Miss Laura.' Beatsie beamed at her happily. 'Now come and sit down and let me do your hair. It's beautiful hair, but you wear it skinned back so tight a person would think you didn't like curly hair.'

From the doorway, Martia asked, 'Do you need any help, Beatsie?'

Without looking up from the task of brushing Miss Laura's surprising luxuriant

153

graying locks, Beatsie said briskly, 'No, thanks. I can cope!'

'If you can't, ring, and somebody will be here on the double,' Martia told her.

'Sure,' said Beatsie, absorbed in twisting Miss Laura's hair into a becoming coiffure.

In the corridor, Martia met Peter, who was emerging from a ward across the hall, scowling as though something troubled him.

'Is Mrs. Hutchens worse?' Martia asked swiftly.

Peter became aware of her, and the scowl was erased by a grin.

'Oh, no, she just demands to attend the wedding, and I'm not quite sure she should,' he answered.

Impulsively Martia protested, 'Oh, but, Doctor, don't you think it might do her good? I mean—well, she's very lonely, and I just thought that being with people, at the wedding—' His look silenced her.

After a moment Peter said briskly, 'You might be right, Nurse.'

Stinging color poured into her face, but she made her eyes meet his and said huskily, 'I'm sorry, Doctor. I didn't mean to question your judgment. It's just that being a woman myself, and knowing that it must be very lonely for her, with her son and his family living in Hawaii where it's very difficult for them to come to see her, I thought that perhaps a wheel chair might not take too

154

much of her strength. I'm sorry.'

Peter had listened, watching her, not taking his eyes off her face. Now he said curtly, 'I'm sure William can find an extra wheel chair for her, though there's quite a run on them with some of the bedridden patients refusing to stay in their beds even if they have to walk! Well, we'll see.'

He turned away and strode down the corridor, and Martia watched him go through a blur of tears.

By three-thirty the solarium was well-filled. The ambulatory patients were disposed about the room, occupying the chairs and settees, and William had brought in the hospital's entire stock of wheel chairs for those who were not ambulatory.

The minister had arrived and was going about the room, greeting the patients and trying not to look at his wrist-watch.

Martia slipped from the room and to Beatsie's door, where she tapped lightly, walked in and stood stock-still before the metamorphosis Beatsie had brought about in Miss Laura.

Miss Laura stood tall and straight, clad in a very becoming frock of a shade that was not quite gray, not quite blue, or even lavender; but a sort of iridescent combination of all three. It fitted her snugly, and the skirt flowed away to the tips of her slippers, that were silver brocade. On her

155

beautifully dressed hair, there was a cap-like hat of violets and lilies of the valley; in her hands was a white and gold prayer book showered with small white wild orchids and lilies of the valley.

Beatsie beamed joyously at Martia and demanded, 'Well?'

'Oh, very well, Beatsie! Why, Miss Laura, you're beautiful!' Martia told her with convincing sincerity.

A tiny tinge of color crept into Miss Laura's cheek beneath the make-up Beatsie had so deftly applied.

'I'm not, really,' she protested breathlessly. 'But this dear child! Beatsie, I can never thank you enough. It's—why, it's a miracle!'

Behind Martia, there was a tap at the door, and Kirby thrust his head in. But before the words on his lips could become speech, he stared at Miss Laura and gave a wolf whistle.

'Well, well, *well*!' he marveled. 'I had no idea I was such a perfect shopper! Form a line at the right, ladies, if you need expert shopping.'

'Expert shopping me eye,' Beatsie sniffed disdainfully. 'Don't let him fool you. All he is is a package picker-upper and a driver with them home. I spent an hour on the telephone with the bridal consultant at Mass Bros. In Tampa, ordering these things. All Kirby did was drive up there yesterday and bring them back. He didn't choose a single thing!'

'Well, I could have,' Kirby pretended to be very hurt, 'only you insisted on doing it all yourself.'

He looked Miss Laura over and nodded with deep satisfaction.

'But I must say my girl friend did a very smashing job. I'd never have been able to select anything so exactly right, Miss Laura. I have to give the girl credit. And to think it was all over the telephone, too!'

He looked at Beatsie with owl-eyed respect, and Beatsie grinned at him and wrinkled her nose like a little girl.

'I forgot why I was sent here, Miss Laura,' Kirby told her. 'The festivities await the presence of the bride. So if you're quite ready—'

He bowed, offered his arm and escorted her to the door. There Dr. John was waiting, and he, too, had a startled moment when he was scarcely able to recognize Miss Laura. Then he offered his arm, and they walked down the corridor toward the solarium.

Beatsie gazed after them damply.

'I thought sure she was going to cry when she first saw what she looked like in her wedding finery,' she admitted to Martia and Kirby. 'But I warned her that if she so much as whimpered, I'd slug her!'

Kirby stared at her.

'You know something?' he mused half aloud. 'I bet you would have, too!'

Beatsie, adjusting herself into her spike-heeled slippers, looked up at him, puzzled.

'Well, I'd spent forty minutes on her make-up,' she told him. 'Did you think I was going to let her go all weepy and ruin my work?'

She brushed her hands, took off the hospital gown that she had swung around her shoulders while she worked on Miss Laura, and stood revealed in a very becoming jade-green frock.

'Well, shall we go?' she suggested brightly, and slipped her hand through Kirby's arm, smiling up at him.

Kirby looked down at her, as his free hand covered the one she had tucked through the crook of his arm, and said softly, a thoughtful look in his eyes, 'I don't suppose we could make this a double wedding, could we?'

Beatsie's blue eyes flew wide, and she caught her breath on a small soundless gasp before she stammered, 'But of course we could, easy as anything.' And then she caught herself, and her voice steadied. 'Only of course you are only kidding.'

Kirby answered cautiously, 'Well, I suppose I am.'

'Then don't!' Beatsie snapped. 'Making

me look and feel ridiculous is so easy it's unworthy of you. It's like shooting a mosquito with an elephant gun.'

She turned to Martia, and there was a strange brightness in her eyes that despised the easy solace of tears.

'Come on, Martia; we don't want to be late for the festivities,' she said curtly. 'They won't wait for us, you know. We aren't important enough.'

She sailed out into the corridor, disengaging her hand from Kirby's arm, her head held high as she walked. And Martia and Kirby followed her, Kirby watching her with a curiously speculative glance that made Martia's mouth curl in a small, knowing smile.

As they reached the solarium, Dr. John and Laura were in place before the improvised altar, and Jason, too, stood there, leaning heavily on his cane.

The minister smiled at them, cleared his throat and began, 'Dearly beloved, we are gathered here—' the lovely, old words that no amount of repetition can ever make stale or routine. And when he reached the place where he asked, 'Who giveth this woman to be married to this man?' Dr. John smiled down at Miss Laura, took her hand from his arm, laid it in Jason's, said firmly, 'I do,' and stepped back.

Jason's hand closed on Miss Laura's, and

together they faced the minister for the balance of the ceremony. And when it was over, and the minister said, 'You may kiss the bride,' Jason was as awkward as a schoolboy on his first date.

Watching, feeling a mist rise in her eyes, Martia turned her head toward where she knew Peter Hayden was standing, expecting to meet his eyes. Instead, Peter was standing beside Elena, looking down at her, smiling into her lifted eyes as she murmured something to him. Then both turned to offer congratulations to Jason and Miss Laura.

Martia drew a long hard breath as she slipped from the solarium. She was on duty, and some of the patients had not been able to attend the wedding. As she passed from the room, a cook, wearing an enormous white cap that towered above his dark, smiling face, was wheeling in a cart carrying a big, very elaborate wedding cake, and Bill's camera was busy.

Martia went about the wards and the private rooms where those patients who hadn't been able to attend the wedding were waiting eagerly to hear about it. When she had visited them all, checked their charts and satisfied their curiosity, she came back to the solarium.

The ambulatory patients were still clustered about the cart on which the wedding cake was being sliced and served.

Miss Laura and Jason were being smiled on and congratulated and fussed over and were obviously enjoying every minute. But there was no sign of Peter or of Elena.

Her heart slid down, but she kept her head high and chatted with the people about her. When Kirby made his way toward her, she was in a little oasis of silence in a corner.

Kirby grinned warmly at her.

'Quite a to-do, wasn't it? Beautifully stage-managed, I call it,' he told her. 'Whoever made the arrangements should take a bow.'

'It was a lovely wedding, wasn't it?' Martia agreed.

Kirby's brows drew together in a slight frown and he said quietly, 'You probably made the arrangements yourself, and now you're whipped down, and no wonder.'

'I only helped a bit,' Martia interrupted him. 'I think Beatsie deserves more credit than anyone else, for doing such a transformation on Miss Laura.'

Kirby beamed happily. 'She really did a job, didn't she?'

'She did, indeed!'

'She's really quite a gal!'

Martia's tired eyes held a faint twinkle.

'Careful, Kirby!' she mocked.

He looked startled, and then he grinned. 'I nearly put my foot in it earlier, didn't I?'

Martia asked quietly, 'Would that have

been so bad, Kirby?'

'D'you know something?' Kirby was giving his answer considerable thought. 'I'm beginning to wonder.'

Martia waited, and suddenly Kirby's tone altered, became briskly matter of fact.

'I have Dr. John's permission to take the child out to dinner, and we wondered if you would care to come along. We hoped you would.'

Martia's mouth curved in a tiny smile, and there was a faintly derisive gleam in her eyes.

'*Hoped* I would? Oh, come now, Kirby!' she mocked him. 'Since when have you needed a chaperone on your dates?'

Kirby grinned an acknowledgement of the thrust.

'Oh, I'm sure I can find a date for you if you'll come,' he assured her.

'Well, thanks, but I am a bit tired,' Martia told him, and smothered a smile as he could not quite keep the relief from showing in his eyes. 'Ask me again sometime.'

Beatsie was weaving her way through the crowded room. As she reached them, Kirby looked down at her and said, 'Martia's too tired to go out to dinner with us.'

Beatsie beamed at Martia and, leaning close, brushed Martia's cheek with her lips and murmured in her ear, 'Thanks pal! Thanks a whole heap! You're a livin' doll!'

She turned to Kirby, thrust her hand

162

through his arm and said briskly, 'Leave us take our foot in our hand and travel, boy! I'm starving to death by inches!'

'Not too late, Beatsie. Have her back by bed-check, Kirby! She's still a patient, remember!' Martia called after them.

Over his shoulder, Kirby grinned at her and winked.

'Yessum,' he said docilely.

Martia smiled as she saw them walk out, Beatsie moving with the slightly awkward step she had not yet lost but would soon; Kirby beaming down at her happily.

Martia was unaware of Dr. John's presence until he spoke at her elbow.

'I suppose that may be our next wedding?' he suggested, nodding toward Kirby and Beatsie, who were walking out of the solarium.

'Oh, I'm afraid not, Dr. John,' Martia protested. 'I have an idea that the minute we dismiss her, she will head for some place much more exciting than Sunset Acres.'

Dr. John scowled.

'Do you now?' he mused. 'We'll be letting her go in a few more days, and I understand she has taken a room at the Inn and will stay on, at least for the summer.'

'I didn't know that!' Martia responded and added, 'I really am surprised.'

Dr. John chuckled.

'Oh, come now, Martia,' he teased her.

163

'Surely you must have seen how things were going with her. Why, you have only to notice the way she blooms when she sees Kirby or even hears his voice. And I have a hunch that young man, who has been as wary of marriage as a shot bird dog, is about to go the route almost any time now!'

He grinned at Martia's startled look and turned as a patient demanded his attention, leaving Martia with a good deal to think about as she went out to supervise the supper trays.

CHAPTER ELEVEN

It was hard for both the staff and the patients to settle down after the excitement of the wedding. They discussed it endlessly, the patients and the aides especially.

Now that Miss Laura had become Mrs. Jason Weathersbee and had moved into Jason's handsome Mediterranean bungalow, she had less time for the hospital, and she apologized every time she came in.

'It's not as though I had a lot of work to do,' she explained to Martia pridefully. 'Jason's man is simply wonderful. And the house is *so* easy to care for. It's just that Jason doesn't like me to leave him for any length of time.'

Martia smiled warmly. 'Well, of course not. He's got a lot of loneliness to get rid of. And so have you. I'm so happy for you, Miss Laura.'

Miss Laura said huskily, her eyes filling with tears, 'I never dreamed, Martia, that anything like this could happen to me. It's a blessed miracle!'

She blew her nose, mopped her damp eyes and asked eagerly, 'Is Beatsie all right?'

'Beatsie's just fine. She is leaving tomorrow,' Martia answered.

Miss Laura cried out, stricken, 'Oh, no! Oh, she mustn't!'

Puzzled, Martia said, 'But, Miss Laura, she is quite well, and she naturally wants to go.'

Miss Laura looked frightened and badly shaken.

'Oh, but I'd counted on her to help me assemble a wardrobe that Jason will like.' She looked down disapprovingly at the dark print dress she was wearing. 'He thought I looked nice in my wedding dress. And now, when he sees the kind of clothes I have always worn before—well, I just can't take a chance on him being sorry he married me.'

'Oh, now, Miss Laura, you mustn't say that. You know he never will be,' Martia tried to console her.

'Well, we went to dinner at the Lodge the other night, and I wore the best dress I had.

Not my wedding dress, of course, but my "Sunday-go-to-meeting" dress. And I could see him looking around the room and noticing how smart some of the women looked and how pretty their clothes were. Jason's not a fool, you know.'

Startled, Martia said, 'I'm sure nobody ever thought he was.'

'Well, anyway, maybe Beatsie can help me get a few things together before she leaves. May I go in and see her?'

'Of course, Miss Laura. I'm sure she'll be delighted to see you,' Martia answered.

As Miss Laura walked along the corridor, in the neat but very uninspired dark print dress, her unbecoming hat perched on top of her gray hair, Martia told herself that Jason must surely wonder what had happened to that all but dazzling bride he had married. Yet, of course, he had known Miss Laura as she was now a lot longer than he had known her as a bride. But being a woman, she could understand exactly how Miss Laura felt in her definitely unglamorous wardrobe.

Shortly before lunch time, Martia looked up to see Kirby approaching the nurses' station, beaming happily.

'I've come to spring one of your patients, Martia,' he announced. 'Let down the drawbridge over the moat and bring out the captive princess.'

Martia laughed at him. 'Meaning Beatsie,

166

of course?'

'Who else?' he agreed happily. 'I had a phone call from her, and it seems I'm wanted.' He paused thoughtfully and added, 'And isn't that a pleasant thought?'

Martia twinkled at him demurely. 'I'm sure it must be. You know where to find her.'

'Yessum,' said Kirby, and was unexpectedly serious for a moment. 'Yes, I know where to find her. And that's as pleasant a thought as a guy could hope to have, isn't it?'

And without waiting for her to answer, he strode off down the corridor toward room 329. Within a matter of minutes, he emerged from the room with Beatsie, wearing a crisply immaculate blue frock that almost matched her eyes, her golden hair held back from her lovely face by a wide matching ribbon. Her hand rested lightly on his arm, although he had no real need for such support, since she had been walking anywhere she liked ever since shortly before the wedding.

'Kirby's taking me to lunch, and then we are going sight-seeing,' she burbled happily at Martia.

'Well, don't let her drive, Kirby,' Martia warned.

'She's never going to drive again,' said Kirby firmly. And as Beatsie lifted outraged

167

eyes and drew her breath for a scathing
answer, he added hastily, 'That is, not as
long as I have anything to say about it.'

'And just who ever gave you the
preposterous, utterly fantastic, completely
incredible, not to say cockeyed idea that
you'll ever have anything to say about
anything I do?' she demanded.

Kirby looked properly abashed and said,
'Sorry, Princess! I guess I just got carried
away with the thought that something
unpleasant might happen to you if you were
driving.'

Beatsie sniffed disdainfully and walked
out; Kirby winked at Martia over his
shoulder as he followed her.

Peter Hayden, coming down the corridor,
saw them go and paused at the nurses'
station, watching them.

'The girl's made a marvelous recovery!' he
commented. 'The night they brought her in
here, I wouldn't have given a plugged nickel
for her chances of ever walking again.'

'She's had superb medical care, Doctor,'
Martia reminded him. He turned and looked
down at her, and though his brows were
drawn in a slight scowl, his eyes held the
ghost of a twinkle.

'I'm sure Dr. John and I both appreciate
that a great deal,' he told her, a faintly
mocking tone in his voice. 'But she has also
had the finest possible nursing care. So he

168

and I can't take all the credit.'

'I'll be sorry to see her go,' Martia admitted impulsively, and added hastily, 'oh, I'm delighted she's able to leave. It's just that having a patient as young and pretty as she is is a—well, a break in the routine.'

Peter, studying her, asked with a quiet earnestness that surprised her, 'Are you tired of caring for geriatrics, Martia?'

'Of course not,' Martia answered quite sincerely. 'It's just that there is so little we can do for them. They have so little to build from, and some of them just don't care. A girl like Beatsie has all her life ahead of her, and is so determined to get well, to resume that life. Now she has, and I'm glad for her. But I'll miss her, too.'

Peter nodded, and now he was as serious as she.

'I'll miss her, too,' he confessed. 'But you and I have considerable life ahead of us, if we don't fool around and waste it and wind up like the others here—unwanted, unloved and unsung.'

He smiled faintly at her startled look and walked away.

Martia drew a deep, hard breath. Absurdly, she remembered something she had overheard one day when a group of aides were working in the dispensary under her careful supervision. One girl was saying sadly, 'Oh, he's a dream boat, a real dream boat! But he keeps drifting away. Just when you think you've got him where you want him, he gives you a grin and walks away.'

The girls had become aware of Martia's presence and guiltily stopped their chatter. But the words had come back to Martia several times since. And now it seemed to her every time Dr. Peter Hayden stayed long enough in her presence to become serious, he walked away or was called away.

She sighed and tried to tell herself it didn't really matter. But she knew she was lying. It mattered a very great deal, because now, as surely as she knew she was alive, she knew she loved him! Derek's memory would always be warm and sweet in her heart. But Peter Hayden held the key to that heart, and it was swept and polished and waiting for him to turn the key and enter in to take complete possession.

It was late afternoon when Kirby and Beatsie returned, and Beatsie was aglow with excitement.

'Martia, I'm going to open a shop in Sunset Acres, for women like Miss Laura who aren't satisfied with the ugly things the local shops think are right for women in their "golden years." And I wonder whatever clown thought of that phrase?' She was burbling eagerly as she reached the nurses' station where Martia was going over the charts. 'Anyway, Kirby's found me a darling little shop I can rent, and I'm going to stock things like Miss Laura likes, and I bet it'll be a wow of a success!'

Startled, Martia looked sharply at her.

'You're planning to stay on in Sunset Acres?' she asked. 'Indefinitely?'

Beatsie grinned joyously and flicked a glance at Kirby.

'Permanently,' she insisted, 'from now on! Oh, I know they won't sell me a house or an apartment here in the Acres, not until I'm a toothless old hag. But Kirby knows a place outside the limits of the Acres where I can go and live.'

Kirby said pleasantly, 'It's my house.'

Martia's eyes widened.

'You're moving out to let her have the place, Kirby?' she asked.

Kirby grinned. 'Oh, no. She's moving in with me.'

Martia looked from one to the other, and Beatsie gave a little delighted peal of laughter.

'I'm marrying the guy!' she announced gaily.

'What?' gasped Martia, and looked swiftly at the beaming Kirby.

'She finally wore me down,' he said modestly.

Beatsie laughed, looking up at him with adoring eyes, her face flushed, her whole manner one of such ecstatic bliss that Martia

171

was deeply touched.

'And don't think I didn't have my work cut out for me!' Beatsie said happily. 'But he didn't really have a chance to escape from me, not from the very first minute he walked into my room and wanted to interview me. I knew then that I wanted to marry him, so I kept slugging away. And finally I wore him down.'

Martia said, before she could control the words, 'Kirby, are you *very* sure?'

Before he could answer, Beatsie protested sharply, 'Hey, wait a minute. Are you trying to talk him out of it?'

'Of course not,' Martia said with slightly guilty haste. 'I'm very happy for both of you. But you haven't known each other very long, and I wondered if you were both quite sure that this is what you really want.'

Beatsie laughed, but her eyes that met Kirby's caressing gaze were warm and tender.

'I was never so sure of anything in my life,' she said softly.

'Nor was I.' Kirby's tone matched hers, as he put his arm about her and drew her close for a moment.

Martia said with an effort at lightness that did not quite come off, 'Too bad you didn't decide a couple of weeks ago while the solarium was still flower-decorated and fresh from the Weathersbee wedding.'

Beatsie said instantly, 'Oh, we're not planning to be married here at the hospital. We thought we'd drive out to someplace where there is a quaint, old-fashioned church dating back two or three hundred years and be married there. Then in years to come we can take our children there and say, "There, dears! Right in front of that altar was where Papa promised to love, honor and obey Mama!"'

Outraged, Kirby protested, 'It's you who are supposed to obey me, my girl. And don't you forget it.'

Beatsie laughed at him and said to Martia, 'Poor sweet! He has an awful lot to learn, hasn't he? But leave it to me. I'll learn him!'

'That's what you think,' Kirby protested, but the warmth in his eyes gave the lie to the would-be sternness in his tone.

Beatsie turned back to Martia and said, 'We want you and Dr. Hayden to be our witnesses. Will you?'

'I can only speak for myself, Beatsie, but I'll be delighted.' Martia told her. 'I'm sure if you ask Dr. Hayden, he will be glad to "stand up" with you.'

Beatsie eyed her curiously for a moment. Then Kirby said briskly, 'Well, you'll see him before I will, honey-chile, so you ask him. Now I've got to toddle along. I do have a business to run, you know.'

'Of course, sweetie,' Beatsie said warmly.

173

'I'll be here in the morning to drive you over to the Inn as soon as Dr. Hayden dismisses you,' Kirby told her, and Martia knew they had forgotten her presence and turned away. Yet she heard Kirby say very softly, 'I love you very much, honey.'

And Beatsie's answer, soft, shaken with ardor, was: 'And I love you very much, darling. Oh, if you could only know how I have *ached* to hear you say that.'

'I'll say it to you twenty-four hours a day, seven days a week, for the rest of my life,' Kirby promised her recklessly.

Martia did not turn back to face them until she heard Kirby walking across the lobby toward the exit. Then she found Beatsie watching him, a lovely smile curling her soft mouth, her eyes shining.

'Isn't he wonderful?' Beatsie breathed. 'I'm the luckiest girl in the world to have snagged him. Just suppose my car hadn't smashed up here! I might never have met him! And that would be the most awful thing that could have happened to me!'

Martia asked after a moment. 'When is the wedding, Beatsie?'

'Oh, a week from today,' Beatsie answered, and grinned impishly. 'I can't take a chance on his changing his mind, you know. I worked too hard to get him to let him escape now.'

'I'm sure you don't have to worry about

that,' Martia laughed. 'In fact, I'll tell you a little secret. He was attracted to you from the very first time he met you.'

Beatsie beamed at her joyously. 'He was? And I was so hateful!'

'Well, you've changed quite a bit, Beatsie,' Martia reminded her.

Beatsie nodded soberly. 'Mellowed, you mean? That's what Kirby calls it. I guess maybe I have. I'd like to think so. Having somebody to love and somebody who loves you makes a person feel mellow, don't you think?'

'I'm sure of it,' Martia answered.

Beatsie straightened and drew a deep hard breath.

'We're flying to New York on our honeymoon, and I'm going to shop for things for the new place I'm going to open,' she boasted happily.

Martia said, almost before she was aware of her intention, 'Beatsie, while you are in New York, will you do me a favor?'

Beatsie said eagerly, 'Of course, Martia. Name it and consider it done.'

'Go and see your father.'

Beatsie stared at her, outraged.

'Are you out of your mind? Now why would I go to see the old man?' she gasped. 'I feel about him just the way I did when I came here, only more so!'

'Beatsie, you should make peace with

him,' Martia urged earnestly.

For the moment Beatsie was more like the Beatsie whom Martia had met in the beginning.

'Make peace with him? For Pete's sake, why?' she snapped. 'He hates me as much as I hate him. He wants to see me just as little as I want to see him. And believe me, that's so little it doesn't bear thinking about.'

'But wouldn't you like him to meet Kirby, his son-in-law?'

That was a question that stopped Beatsie in her tracks, and for a moment she looked a trifle shaken, even bewildered. Then an impish grin touched her mouth, and there was a twinkle in her eyes, so big and so blue that they were like cornflowers.

'Come to think of it,' she admitted after a moment's thought, 'that could be fun, at that. Maybe Kirby'll take a poke at him if he gets as nasty as he usually does at sight of me.'

'Oh, I'm sure he won't,' Martia protested.

Beatsie's chuckle was grimly unamused.

'You don't know my old man,' she drawled. 'From as far back as I can remember, he was always warning me that a man wouldn't fall in love with *me* as a woman, but with the Conrad money! But he can't say Kirby's a fortune-hunter, because I am no longer the heiress to the Conrad money, praises be. I was cut off with the

176

proverbial shilling—except for the money my mother left in trust for me and that I'm going to use to open the shop.'

There were footsteps along the corridor, and Peter Hayden, completing his afternoon rounds, approached the nurses' station. Seeing him, Beatsie dropped the thought of her father for the moment and addressed herself to Peter.

'Well, hello,' Peter greeted her pleasantly. 'You're looking full of vim and vigor. What have you been up to?'

Beatsie beamed at him joyously.

'Out hunting a place to open a shop, and getting myself engaged,' she announced happily, and rushed on, 'Dr. Hayden, would you be best man at my wedding?'

'I'd be honored,' Peter answered. 'Dare I ask the name of the fortunate young man?'

Beatsie's brows went up in slight surprise at such a question.

'Why, it's Kirby, of course,' she answered. 'Who else could it be?'

For an instant Peter's eyes flickered toward Martia, and then he asked unnecessarily, 'Kirby Clarke?'

Puzzled, Beatsie asked, 'Well, who else?'

'It's quite true you haven't had much chance to meet other eligible young men since you've been here, have you?' he agreed thoughtfully.

Beatsie's eyes flashed, and her jaw

tightened.

'Are you trying to say I am marrying Kirby just because there is nobody else available?' she flashed hotly. 'Because if you are, Dr. Hayden, I don't think I want you as Kirby's best man! Kirby's the only man I could ever want to marry, and now that I've got him, nothing and nobody is going to separate us, not even my old man!'

'Hey, now, wait a minute,' Peter protested, laughing. 'Simmer down, girl! I just thought Kirby had—well, shall we say other plans?'

He did not so much as glance at Martia, but she felt color sting her cheeks, because she knew only too well what he meant.

'Well if he ever had any other plans, he'd better get rid of them, and quick!' Beatsie said belligerently. 'I put my brand on him the very first day I set eyes on him, and every day since then *my* plans for him have been getting stronger and stronger! And now I've gotten him to ask me. I was a maiden very shy who said sweetly, "This is *so* sudden!" just as they do in the story books. And Kirby just laughed and said, "You blessed idiot, I knew you would say that!"'

She chuckled fondly at the memory and then became brisk once more.

'We have to have two witnesses. Martia has agreed to be one, so if you'll be the other, Doctor, we'll be very grateful!'

Peter gave her a slight bow, smiled down at her and said firmly, 'It will be an honor and a privilege, Miss Conrad.'

'Thank you, Doctor. You're sweet!'

'You're very welcome.' Peter asked, 'I suppose you're planning to be married here?'

'Oh, good grief, no!' Beatsie protested. And then as though unwilling to give offense, she added hastily, 'I've always wanted to be married in a church!'

'I see. One of the Sunset Acres churches?'

'Um, no.' Beatsie was still unwilling to give offense. 'We thought it would be nice to drive north somewhere along the coast until we found a church all nestled in hibiscus and palm trees, with an orange grove somewhere near by!'

'That sounds very romantic,' Peter agreed, a twinkle in his eyes.

'Well, we want it to be romantic,' Beatsie insisted. 'After all, our entire courtship has been here in the hospital. And while it's a very nice hospital, and Miss Laura's wedding was lovely, we thought we'd like to change to some other place.'

Peter nodded, and Beatsie went on, 'So if you and Martia will go with us and sign the register or do whatever witnesses do at a wedding, Kirby and I will appreciate it very much.'

Peter glanced at Martia, whose eyes were downcast, and said warmly, 'I'm sure Martia

179

and I will be very happy to be of whatever service we can, won't we, Martia?'

'Of course,' Martia answered. 'I've already told Beatsie I'd be glad to be her maid of honor.'

'You're a couple of the best!' Beatsie told them happily. 'Well, I'll go finish my packing, since I'm to be transferred to the Inn tomorrow.'

She beamed at both of them and walked away.

When the door closed behind her, Peter turned to Martia and studied her curiously.

'It's almost traditional, isn't it?' he commented mildly.

Puzzled, and not at all sure she liked the look in his eyes, Martia asked, 'What is?'

'The bride's maid of honor being a girl in love with the groom,' he said flatly. 'I've always wondered why brides, some of them very kind and gentle people otherwise, should get such a kick out of the tradition.'

'Perhaps because, as in this case, the maid of honor cares absolutely nothing for the groom, as I've told you many times,' Martia said hotly.

He nodded, the odd enigmatic look still in his eyes as they met her own.

'So you have, so you have,' he agreed mildly. 'Yet I happen to know you did your very best to talk him out of marrying Beatsie.'

180

'That was because I didn't think they were right for each other,' Martia protested.

'And you do now?' He seemed only politely interested, yet his eyes were dark, probing.

Martia's chin went up a little, and her eyes chilled slightly.

'Now that Beatsie has, as she herself expressed it, mellowed, yes!' There was a defensive, almost defiant note in her voice. 'As she was when she first came here, she would have destroyed Kirby. But as she is now, I believe they can be very happy together.'

Peter nodded and was silently thoughtful for a moment. And then he smiled wryly and said, 'Well, we'd better hang out a shingle on the hospital. Two marriages within a few weeks of each other! Quite a record, isn't it?'

'Quite,' she told him levelly.

For a moment they exchanged glances. Then a buzzer summoned Martia, and she went swiftly down the corridor, leaving him standing there.

CHAPTER TWELVE

Because after their wedding, Kirby and Beatsie would be driving to Miami to board a plane for New York, Peter and Martia followed them in Peter's car.

Beatsie was lovely and radiant, as any bride should be on her wedding day, in a soft white frock and a wide-brimmed flower-laden hat, and an orchid riding proudly on her shoulder. Kirby was the usual proud, slightly apprehensive groom. As Peter and Martia followed them, Martia said, 'They make a very attractive couple, don't they?'

It was, she knew, an inane remark, but at least it broke the silence that had lain between them since she had entered his car at the hospital.

'And you make a very attractive maid of honor, Martia,' he told her, and glanced at her in a sleeveless pale pink linen frock, a matching hat of pink roses crowning her head, white gloves and slippers and a large white bag completing her ensemble. 'And if you'll look in that box on the seat there, you'll find a little something I thought you might like to have.'

Martia opened the box and caught her breath at the beauty of the small nosegay of violets centered with one exquisite, half open pink rosebud.

'Like it?' asked Peter, though her expression had already told him that she did, very much. 'They told me at the flower shop that it would go with any other color you chose to wear. I hope it does.'

'It's lovely!' Martia's voice was not entirely

182

steady as she held the small, lace-framed corsage in her two hands.

'Good! I'm not much good at picking pretties for girls,' he admitted, and for the moment seemed more like himself. 'I guess I haven't had much experience, if it comes to that! I'm not like Kirby, who seems to know instinctively just what every woman likes.'

Martia drew a deep breath, and her hands clenched on the small, exquisite nosegay before she said through her teeth, 'Would you do me a very great favor, Dr. Hayden?'

He looked at her cautiously, and then his eyes swung back to the road and ascertained that Kirby's car was still in sight ahead of them.

'If I can,' he agreed cautiously.

'It should be very easy,' she told him, still speaking through her clenched teeth. 'It's just that you remove that note of acerbity out of your voice when you speak to me of Kirby Clarke.'

She saw a small grin tug at the corners of his mouth. But when he spoke his voice was quite serious, his manner mildly puzzled.

'A note of acerbity? Are you going to tell me what that means, or do I have to wait until I get back to the hospital to consult a dictionary?'

'You know perfectly well what I, as well as the word, mean,' she said. 'I mean that any time you mention his name in my presence,

183

you seem to mean a whole heck of a lot more than you say, as if you were laughing at him, or worse still, at me!'

All hint of raillery had vanished from Peter's voice when he said swiftly, 'Not at you, Martia, my dear. Never at you! I could never laugh at you!'

Martia caught her breath and sat very still, not quite daring to look at him.

Ahead of them, Kirby had slowed his car and signaled them. He was turning from the highway along a wide, sandy road bordered on either side by tall palms and blossoming hibiscus. At the end of the road, there was a neat, small white church sitting serenely, as though enjoying its seclusion from the busy highway, along which traffic was a thick and noisy stream.

Kirby's car slipped into a parking space to the left of the church. When Martia and Peter joined him, he and Beatsie were standing beside his car, and Beatsie was looking about her.

'Oh, Martia, isn't it a love of a place? Wouldn't anyone want to be married in such a *lovesome* spot?' she asked happily.

'It's a lovely spot,' Martia agreed. 'But I don't see any sign of a parsonage. Where do you suppose the minister lives? Maybe he just drives out from town for services.'

Before Beatsie could manage an answer, a man came around from the back of the

184

church and peered at them nearsightedly. He wore disreputable trousers, a dark shirt that clung damply to his thin body, and his graying hair was tousled above a face that the Florida sun had tanned to a coppery shade. His hands were grimy with soil; as he approached them, he gave them a gentle, deprecating smile.

'How do you do?' he greeted them formally. 'I'm the Reverend Polk. May I help you?'

Beatsie gasped, 'I thought you were the gardener,' and instantly became scarlet with confusion.

The Reverend Polk laughed gently. 'Oh, I am, my dear. Also the general flunky. But I really am the minister in charge of this church.'

'We're happy to meet you, sir,' Kirby took over. 'I'm Kirby Clarke, and this is my fiancée, Miss Conrad, and we'd like you to marry us, please.'

The frail-looking old man glanced from one to the other, and his blue eyes filled with an innocent delight.

'I shall be very happy to do so.' He beamed at them and then at Peter and Martia and asked, 'Is it a double wedding? You want to be married, too?'

Martia caught her breath and felt hot color sting her cheeks as Peter said pleasantly, 'Well, not at the present moment, sir.

Perhaps later. We are here as witnesses for the happy couple.'

'Oh, I see, I see,' said the old man, and turned once more to Kirby and Beatsie. 'If you will excuse me until I clean up a bit, I'll join you in the church. That is, unless you'd like the ceremony performed in the garden?' He gestured toward the back of the church from which he had first appeared, and they all walked with him around the corner of the church. Beatsie and Martia cried out with delight at sight of the lovely garden there, that was a mass of color and fragrance.

The Reverend Polk was very pleased at their delighted exclamations and left them to admire the garden while he walked down a narrow path to a small house that was half-hidden behind a mass of hibiscus and night-blooming jasmine, with bougainvillaea sprawling across its wall and roofs. Through the dense shrubbery they caught glimpses of the silver-blue of a small, sun-washed lake.

Kirby said, with a deep breath, 'The old gentleman's really got it made. What a place! But you'd think he'd have this beautiful garden out front where people could see it.'

Beatsie shook her head and said softly, 'It's a place for meditation, not for show. You could come here when the whole world seemed determined to lick you, and somehow you'd forget about it while you looked at all this.'

'Then you want the ceremony out here, darling?' asked Kirby.

Beatsie lifted her eyes from the masses of flowers, looked at the little church and shook her head again.

'I'd rather have it there in the church,' she said softly. 'I'll bet it's as beautiful and as peaceful as this lovely garden. I think that's the only kind of church the Reverend Polk would let himself get involved with.'

Across from the garden there was a long rustic bench, and there they sat, delighting in the garden, in the peace and quiet, scarcely speaking as they waited.

The Reverend Polk came hurrying up from the tiny cottage, decently clothed in his somewhat shabby ministerial clothes.

'If you'll just come this way?' He gestured toward a small side door that led directly to the pulpit.

Unexpectedly, Beatsie said, 'We'd rather come through the front door, if you don't mind, and walk down the aisle, hand in hand. I've always thought that's the way I'd like to be married when the time came. And the time is here.' She looked up at Kirby, her eyes warm and tender, and the Reverend Polk cleared his throat a trifle noisily.

'Just as you wish, my dear,' he agreed, and smiled as he walked away from them through the small side door into the church.

Beatsie slipped her hand through Kirby's

arm, and they walked to the front of the church, with Peter and Martia following them. Inside the church, it was dusky and cool. The sunlight found its way through windows that hoped to be mistaken for stained glass, but were only a fairly creditable imitation. On the altar there was a tall glass jar filled with varicolored gladioli that formed an effective background for the Reverend Polk, who stood waiting for them, his well-worn Bible open at the proper page as he watched the four of them walk down the aisle between the shabby pews.

When Beatsie and Kirby reached him, Beatsie looked up at Kirby, and the whole dim old church seemed illuminated by her radiant smile. The Reverend Polk looked at her and then at Kirby and cleared his throat before he began in a surprisingly sonorous voice to read the ancient words.

Martia and Peter, standing behind the two, listened as though they had never heard the words before. And Martia told herself that was because no matter how many times you heard them, they always seemed different and a little more beautiful.

When the ceremony was over, and the minister had pronounced Kirby and Beatsie man and wife, he offered a brief and very touching prayer for their happiness and walked with the four of them out of the church and into the brilliant sunlight.

Beatsie said, her voice unsteady, 'I don't know how to thank you, sir.'

The Reverend Polk said gently, 'You have, my dear, you have. It's always a great joy for me to officiate at a ceremony that brings together two young people so obviously in love.'

Kirby shook hands with him, and a small envelope found its way from Kirby's hands to the old man. The minister looked a trifle startled and protested, 'This isn't at all necessary, Mr. Clarke. It's my pleasure, and one I get very seldom.'

'And mine, sir, so you must let me have my pleasure, too,' Kirby told him.

Beatsie said unsteadily, 'We'll bring our children here to church, sir.'

Momentarily startled, the old man smiled, and there was a twinkle in the faded blue eyes.

'Please do, my dear! I shall look forward to it,' he told her.

He stood on the steps as they walked to the two cars. But when they turned to wave at him, he had already turned and was going back into the church.

Beatsie said, 'Now that was a wedding to remember!'

With an attempt at raillery, Kirby said sternly, 'Well, see that you do, my girl.'

But Beatsie had turned to Martia and was embracing her, saying huskily, 'Martia, I'm going to take Kirby to meet my old man when we get to New York, as you said I should.'

'Beatsie, I'm so glad!' Martia answered, genuinely pleased.

'I want to show Kirby to my old man, and prove to him that I can find myself a husband who is fine and decent and worth-while and honest and upright.'

'Hey, now wait a minute,' Kirby protested with a slight scowl. 'I'm not sure I can live up to half of that.'

Beatsie flung him a cool glance and said serenely, 'Oh, I'll see that you do, darling.'

Kirby stared at her and then at Peter and asked, 'What have I gotten myself into?'

Peter grinned. 'Don't ask me, fella. It was your idea.'

'Well, not entirely,' Beatsie insisted unashamedly. 'Give me part of the credit.'

Kirby eyed her for a moment; then he chuckled and slipped his hand through her arm and guided her toward his car. Over her shoulder Beatsie called, 'Thanks for being with us. You're to be our first dinner guests the very minute I learn to cook!'

Martia and Peter laughed, and Martia called, 'Goodbye, good luck, and God bless you!'

And Beatsie, settling into the car as close to Kirby as she could get, answered radiantly, 'Oh, He already has!'

190

Kirby waved as the car slid down the wide, sandy road. After a moment Peter said politely to Martia, 'And now shall we get going? I thought we might have time for lunch on the way back to the Acres.'

And very sedately, Martia said, 'That would be nice.'

But if she had any idea that his conversation would be affected even mildly by the romantic interlude just concluded, she was doomed to disappointment. For throughout the delectable meal in the hotel at Sarasota, he talked very casually about hospital matters, and there was no indication whatever that he considered her anything more than a casual date.

Back at the hospital, he let her out at the dormitory, and she said politely, 'Thank you, Doctor, for a very pleasant afternoon.'

'I enjoyed it, too,' he told her. 'I've heard these things are contagious, but I don't think any cure has ever been found for it.'

And without giving her a chance to answer, he drove on to the hospital parking lot, leaving her to go in to her room and change from the pink frock to her uniform.

She looked at the lovely nosegay corsage for a long time before at last she drew a deep, uneven breath and laid it gently away in the top drawer of her dresser.

CHAPTER THIRTEEN

Once the two weddings were over, the hospital settled down to routine.

There was a letter from Beatsie to Martia; an ecstatic letter reporting that she and Kirby had gone to see her father, and that her father had welcomed them with such cordiality that it had left her bewildered. He had seemed to know all about Kirby, and was surprised that she should find that unusual. He had assured her that he had been deeply concerned about her, but that he had come to the unwilling conclusion that she was grown up and had the right to live her own life, even to wreck it, if she wanted to. So he had been delighted and surprised to find she had married a man such as Kirby and was even planning to open a shop in a retirement village.

'So you see, Martia darling, you gave me the advice I needed, and now,' she wrote happily, 'everything is just fine. Oh, I don't *love* my old man, and I'm sure he doesn't love me. But at least he isn't ashamed of me any more. And somehow that pleases me a lot! Isn't it funny? I never cared a hang what he or anybody else thought of me. But now that I'm Mrs. Kirby Clarke, I want people to like me, and maybe some day even respect me.'

Martia smiled at the letter and was deeply relieved that Beatsie had been persuaded to make peace with her father. She had felt from the first that, given a chance, the ugly barriers between Beatsie and her father would melt away, and now apparently they had. And she was very glad.

Late that afternoon, going off duty, she saw Peter walking toward the parking lot. On an impulse she did not try to deny, Martia called out to him, and he turned swiftly as she hurried across to him.

'Peter, I want to talk to you,' she told him, and her voice was slightly shaken as she looked up at him.

'Well, of course. What's on your mind?' Peter asked, his voice unexpectedly curt. Martia caught her breath for an instant and then managed a faint smile as she drew Beatsie's letter out of her pocket.

'I just wanted you to know that I've had a letter from Beatsie and she's very happy,' she told him idiotically.

Peter's brows went up ever so slightly.

'Well, that's not so surprising, is it? After all, she married the man she loved.' His tone of voice held a faintly mocking note. 'I'd say Beatsie was a very lucky girl, wouldn't you?'

'She is, of course,' Martia agreed. 'She's made up with her father, and he seems delighted that she has married a man like

Kirby.'

'I can imagine.' The mockery in Peter's tone was a little stronger now, and his eyes probed hers with a sharpness that her own were too misted with tears to recognize. 'There aren't too many fellows like Kirby around these days, as I'm sure you agree.'

Martia drew a deep breath and clenched her fists in the pockets of her uniform as she looked up at him.

'Peter,' she said huskily, 'you told me once that you cared for me.'

She thought he gave a swiftly controlled start, and then he said sharply, 'Not once, but several times. And I didn't say I cared for you; I said I loved you! And you were so busy remembering the past that you couldn't be bothered listening to me.'

'Oh, but, Peter, I was so wrong,' she whispered unsteadily.

Peter stared at her as though he could not quite believe what she was saying. Then he caught her by the shoulders, gave her a by no means gentle shake and demanded sharply, 'What the devil are you trying to say?'

'Don't make me say it, Peter.' There was such utter humility in her voice that for a long moment Peter merely stood there, his hands still on her shoulders, peering down at her beneath knitted brows.

Suddenly, as though he had seen something in her misted eyes that he scarcely dared believe, Peter turned about, swung open the door of his car and said sharply, 'Get in!'

Martia's eyes widened, but she did not move.

'I said to *get in*!' Peter's tone was stiff with authority, and his hand on her arm urged her toward and into the car.

As he slipped beneath the wheel and started the car, Martia stared at him and asked, 'Where are we going?'

'Somewhere where we can have a good long talk and get a whole raft of problems, questions and answers all straightened out,' he told her, and there was nothing even remotely tender or lover-like in his crisp, sharp voice. 'Do you mind?'

'Of course not,' she stammered, and saw the faintest possible smile tugging at the corners of his grimly set mouth.

She sat beside him, hands folded tightly in her lap, eyes on the road ahead, as they drove swiftly to the outskirts of the village and then to the Lodge. Across the wide, sandy road from the Lodge there was a small summerhouse garlanded with bougainvillaea and several benches tucked beside the path. Beyond was the Gulf, lit now with the lovely afterglow of sunset.

Peter swung the car into a parking space, got out, swung the door open on Martia's side, and held out his hand.

'Get out,' he ordered. 'And don't get sassy with me.'

'Yes, sir, Doctor, sir!' Martia had managed to find enough raillery to steady her voice as she walked beside him to the farthermost bench. There he turned and swung her around to face him.

'All right; let's have it,' he demanded. 'Are you trying to tell me you've had a change of heart? And if so, why?'

Martia drew a deep, hard breath and said quietly, 'I have had a change of heart, as you express it. I've found out that my heart is big enough to hold lovely memories of the past, but to grow hungry for present love as well.'

'So?' His tone was noncommittal, but the look in his eyes was hungry, yearning, burning with a hope he scarcely dared acknowledge. 'And when did all this happen?'

Martia said quite honestly, 'When I began to be afraid you were falling in love with Elena.'

Obviously that jolted him, and his frown deepened.

'Elena?' he repeated, as though he had never heard the name before. 'Who the devil is Elena?'

'Elena Marchant.'

As though recalling her identity for the first time since the name had been mentioned, Peter said, his brow clearing,

196

'Oh, that newspaper gal that did the spread about the village and the hospital. I'd say she did a very good job of writing, wouldn't you? I understand the administration office is being swamped with inquiries. He broke off and stared down at her as though not a bit sure he liked her. 'You thought I was falling for *her*?'

'Well, you were giving a very good imitation of it,' Martia told him, her resentment rising beneath his look of shocked amusement.

'My dear girl!' His tone held a gentle, but deeply amused reproof. 'What sort of a fool do you take me for, thinking I could have been swept off my feet by a phony dame like that? I'm not quite a callow youth, you know. I've been in the medical field quite awhile, and I've met quite a few of the likes of her! And I'm still unmarried. I won't say I'm heart-whole and fancy-free, except insofar as Elena Marchant is concerned.'

There was a taut silence between them. A lump in Martia's throat warned her that if she tried to talk she would burst into tears, and she didn't want that. And so she waited, hoping that Peter would help her out. Surely she had gone far enough, had laid her pride low enough for him to pick up the words that now needed so desperately to be said. But he just went on studying her with a curiously speculative look.

'So because you were jealous of Elena—' he began.

'I was *not*,' she protested, but her tone lacked conviction even in her own ears.

'You didn't want me yourself, but you didn't want her to have me.' He accused her. He went on before she could defend herself, 'That's a "dog in the manger" attitude, Martia, and completely unworthy of a girl like you. "I don't want him, but I'm not going to let you have him, either." I'm surprised, Martia.'

'It wasn't—it isn't like that at all!' she exploded. 'It was just that—well, seeing you with her, realizing that she was beautiful and accomplished and sophisticated, all the things I was not, I suddenly realized that if I lost you, then life wouldn't really mean very much to me any more. Just seeing you together helped make up my mind.'

He didn't seem at all pleased with that and merely waited for her to go on.

'Please, Peter, try to understand,' she pleaded.

'Believe me, I am,' he assured her. And now the curtness was gone from his voice, and it carried a wealth of sincerity that was like a warm cloak about her shaking body. 'I have to understand, Martia, for both our sakes. We can't afford to make a mistake about belonging to each other. Because if ever you are mine, Martia, it will be "until death do us part," for I'll never let you go.'

'I wouldn't want you to, Peter,' she told him huskily, 'because it's like that with me, too! That's what I wanted to tell you: that I know now how much I love you, how much I want to belong to you for always.'

Peter said barely above his breath, in a tone of utmost reverence, 'The saints be praised!'

But still he did not touch her, though her body ached with yearning for the touch of his arms about her.

'And Derek?' he asked at last, his voice taut and strained.

Martia drew a deep breath, and her head came up, her eyes meeting his.

'Derek's memory will always be a part of my life,' she told him. 'I couldn't forget him and all the lovely memories, even if I wanted to, and I don't. But Derek is a part of my young girlhood; what I feel for you is a grown-up, mature love that fills my heart and always will.'

Peter said huskily, 'Remember him, darling, of course. I want you to. But that's all in the past. We've got the present and a glorious future to look forward to.'

Martia said unsteadily, 'Will you please marry me?'

Peter's brows went up, and there was a twinkle in his eyes.

'Hey, that's my line,' he protested.

A small smile curved her tremulous mouth, and she said unsteadily, 'Well, one of us had to say it, and it didn't seem that you were going to.'

'Well, give me time, darling! Right now I'm too rocked to be able to do or say anything,' he said, and at last drew her into his arms and held her closely, his cheek against her hair. 'I can't believe that this is really happening, just when I'd given up hope.'

She tilted her face upward, flushed and rosy, and his lips sought and found her own. He tasted the salt of tears on her lips, and lifted his head and stared down at her.

'Why, Precious, you're crying,' he protested.

'Don't mind me,' she stammered, trying hard to manage a laugh. 'I always cry when I'm very happy.'

'But you mustn't, darling. I want you always to be happy, and I'll do my darnedest to bring that about. But I don't want you crying because you're happy.'

Martia managed a small, unsteady laugh.

'Then it's a habit I'll try to kick!' she promised him shakily.

'Well, see that you do.'

'I will try very hard.'

He held her close for a long moment, looking down at her, his warm, ardent eyes taking in every line of her face as though it had not been imprinted on his memory almost since the first time he had set eyes on her.

'I don't know why I should be so blessed,' he murmured at last as though he spoke his thoughts aloud.

'It's I who am blessed, darling,' Martia said softly, 'to have a second chance at loving and being loved when I had given up hope that it could ever happen again.'

'It has happened, darling, and we both know it's for keeps,' said Peter tenderly. Then, suddenly, he straightened. 'And since we are both off duty for the evening, we're going across to the Lodge and have a bang-up celebration dinner to mark the occasion!'

'But are you off duty for the evening?' she wondered, the octopus-like tentacles of the hospital and their duties there reaching out for her even in this moment of utter glory and delight.

He grinned adoringly at her, kissed her and urged her toward the car.

'I'll check in by phone as soon as we get to the Lodge. And if I am not needed, we'll have dinner. If I am, then we'll scoot back to the hospital. But I *am* supposed to be off duty until ten, and then on call if needed. Didn't you check the schedule before you left?'

Martia laughed up at him.

'I did not! I was too anxious to catch up with you before you drove away.'

Tucking her into the car, he bent his head, kissed her ardently and slid beneath the wheel.

'And just when I'd about given up hope you'd ever decide you cared for me!' he said, and beamed at her.

'I guess we both should be grateful that Elena came to the village,' laughed Martia, put her hands up to her disheveled hair and gasped, 'oh, I must look a mess—in uniform, and my face all tear-stained, and my hair standing on end.'

'You couldn't look anything but beautiful, even if you tried,' he assured her handsomely as he ran the car into a parking slot in front of the Lodge.

'Well, if you don't mind—' She flashed him an adoring smile as he helped her out of the car and walked beside her to the steps of the Lodge.

'I don't mind a bit,' he informed her as they walked into the lobby. 'I'll call the hospital first.'

She waited, and when he came back he was scowling.

'Oh, we have to go back,' she read the look in his face as he turned her back toward the steps.

He nodded grimly. 'There's an emergency,' he told her. 'Payson, who is on duty, has panicked, because he isn't as familiar with the job as I am. So we'll have to go back without dinner.'

As the car started, he looked down at her and managed a rueful smile.

'It's a good thing you are a nurse, because you understand these things.'

She smiled at him serenely, slipped her hand through his arm and felt it drawn close to his side as he drove.

'Of course I do,' she said gently. 'There'll be lots of times like this when we'll have to give up some cherished plan because a patient needs you, many times when you'll be late for dinner. But then we have all our lives ahead of us for the plans that won't have to be changed. It's going to be pretty wonderful.'

'With you, any life would be wonderful,' he told her tenderly. 'Without you, nothing would be any good, not even life itself.'

'I know,' she replied, and rested her cheek against his shoulder.

At the hospital, he let her out and turned swiftly toward the emergency entrance without a farewell word to her. But Martia, watching him as he hurried, smiled proudly. For she knew he loved her and he would always come back to her. And after all, that was the only thing that really mattered.

Still smiling that lovely, radiant smile, she turned and walked along the brief narrow path that led to the nurses' dormitory.

F   17.95
Gadd   Curley
Gaddis   LARGE PRINT
Second chance at love

DATE DUE

Apr. 14, 2005	
MAR 0 5 2007	

MD JH EW
PC
Mann

EP
WM

GAYLORD
M2